"You May Kiss The Bride...."

Callen was ready for a quick peck on the lips, but Sam pulled her slowly toward him to claim her mouth. And before he was done, they were both breathing with difficulty.

The judge had a grin on his face. "It's always a pleasure to see two people in love...."

Callen noticed the smile on Sam's lips, but it never reached his eyes. Was it the mention of *love* that bothered him? Sam had never said the word to her, but he had certainly shown her that he cherished her. Besides, this was no time to have second thoughts. The deed was done. She was Mrs. Sam Longstreet.

Dear Reader,

I know this is a hectic time of year. From the moment you cut into that Thanksgiving turkey, to the second midnight chimes on December 31, life is one nonstop *RUSH*. But don't forget to take some private time…and relax with Silhouette Desire!

We begin with *An Obsolete Man,* a marvelous *Man of the Month* from the ever-entertaining Lass Small. Next we have *The Headstrong Bride,* the latest installment in Joan Johnston's CHILDREN OF HAWK'S WAY series.

And there's *Hometown Wedding,* the first book in a fun-filled new series, JUST MARRIED, by Pamela Macaluso, a talented new-to-Desire writer. And speaking of new authors, don't miss Metsy Hingle's debut title, *Seduced.*

This month is completed with *Dark Intentions,* a sensuous, heartwarming love story by Carole Buck, and *Murdock's Family,* a powerfully dramatic offering by Paula Detmer Riggs.

Happy holidays—don't worry, you'll survive them!

Lucia Macro
Senior Editor

Please address questions and book requests to:
Silhouette Reader Service
U.S.: 3010 Walden Ave., P.O. Box 1325, Buffalo, NY 14269
Canadian: P.O. Box 609, Fort Erie, Ont. L2A 5X3

JOAN
JOHNSTON
THE HEADSTRONG BRIDE

SILHOUETTE *Desire*®
Published by Silhouette Books
America's Publisher of Contemporary Romance

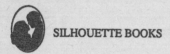 SILHOUETTE BOOKS

ISBN 0-373-05896-9

THE HEADSTRONG BRIDE

Books by Joan Johnston

Silhouette Desire

Fit To Be Tied #424
Marriage by the Book #489
Never Tease a Wolf #652
A Wolf in Sheep's Clothing #658
A Little Time in Texas #710
Honey and the Hired Hand #746
*The Rancher and the Runaway Bride #779
*The Cowboy and the Princess #785
*The Wrangler and the Rich Girl #791
*The Cowboy Take a Wife #842
+The Unforgiving Bride #878
+The Headstrong Bride #896

*Hawk's Way
+Children of Hawk's Way

JOHN JOHNSTON

started reading romances to escape the stress of being an attorney with a major national law firm. She soon discovered that writing romances was a lot more fun than writing legal bond indentures. Since then, she has published a number of historical and contemporary category romances. In addition to being an author, Joan is the mother of two children. In her spare time, she enjoys sailing, horseback riding and camping.

For Priscilla Kelley
Because the little things do matter

Prologue

"I'm so sorry about your father." Callen Whitelaw felt awkward offering sympathy to someone she hardly knew. At first she didn't think the grieving man was going to reply. When he did, he said one word in a ragged whisper.

"Thanks."

Callen tried to imagine Sam Longstreet crying with enough despair to make himself hoarse. She wanted to fold him in her arms and comfort him. But he was a stranger, even though he had been a neighbor all her life. She had known his father, E.J., better than she knew Sam, because E.J. had come to Hawk's Way often to spend time with her father.

"Is there anything I can do?" she asked.

"No." He hesitated a moment, then said, "Maybe there is. I have to go to Amarillo on business. Maybe you could meet me there, have dinner with me. I...I could use the company."

Callen was stunned by the invitation, which seemed to come out of the blue. Why would Sam Longstreet want to have dinner with her when he didn't even know her?

"Never mind," he said when she hesitated too long.

She caught his arm as he started to turn away. "Wait. Please. I'll be glad to meet you. Just tell me when and where."

He named a time and a restaurant, and then his attention was drawn by another rancher offering condolences.

Callen thought about the invitation during the entire drive home with her family, wondering what had compelled Sam to reach out to her. Once she was home, she asked her eldest brother, Zach, about Sam. Zach admitted to only a passing acquaintance with Sam. Her other brother, Falcon, hadn't come home for the funeral from his ranch in Dallas, but Zach said he could speak for both of them.

"Neither of us knew Sam very well," Zach said. "He was two years ahead of me in school, three years ahead of Falcon, so we didn't have any classes together."

Zach was thirty-four, so that would make Sam thirty-six, Callen figured. He had seemed every bit of that, his features chiseled by wind and weather, his striking green eyes webbed at the corners by the sun, his wide mouth bracketed by lines, his shaggy, chestnut hair streaked with blonde. It was a face aged by the hard life of a Texas rancher and by the grief that sat upon his brow.

"Sam wasn't too good with the books," Zach continued. "The football coach got tutors to help him pass his class work so he could play. He was a great running back, as I recall, but he pretty much kept to himself."

"Was he good enough to play professionally?" Callen asked.

"He hurt his knee in the state championship game. I guess he couldn't run fast enough after that to compete in college. He settled in to work on the Double L after high school, and as far as I know he never aspired to anything else. Why are you interested in Sam Longstreet, anyway?"

"He seemed so sad," Callen said.

"Stay away from him," Zach warned. "He's a saddle tramp with a rundown ranch."

"That's unfair!" Callen retorted in defense of a man she had just met. "Just because the Longstreets don't have as much money as the Whitelaws doesn't make Sam any less of a man.''

''He's never going to amount to anything.''

''How do you know?''

''If he was going to do anything with that ranch to improve it, he would have done it by now,'' Zach said.

''Not necessarily,'' Callen retorted. ''Maybe he and his father disagreed about what ought to be done.'' Callen knew she had hit a sore spot with Zach, because he and their father often disagreed about ranching methods.

''You're speculating,'' Zach accused.

''You're just mad because you know I'm right,'' Callen shot back.

Her quarrel with Zach was loud enough to bring their mother, Candy, into the parlor from the kitchen.

''What's going on in here?'' she asked.

''Callen's got herself into a snit over that good-for-nothing at the Double L.''

''Sam Longstreet is not—''

''That's enough from both of you,'' Candy interrupted. ''Zach, don't you have some business with your father in his office?'' Once Zach was gone, she turned to Callen. ''Now what's all this about Sam Longstreet?''

"I spoke to him at E.J.'s funeral," Callen said. "He seemed so alone, Mom, and so sad. I wanted to do something for him, but I didn't know what. He mentioned he was going to be in Amarillo on business and asked me to join him for dinner. I said yes."

Her mother arched a questioning brow but said nothing either to approve or disapprove of what Callen had done.

Yet Callen felt the need to explain herself. "I couldn't say no, Mom. I mean, there was something so peculiar about the way he looked at me. He didn't say much of anything, but I could hear him speaking to me with his eyes. It was so strange."

"Peculiar. Strange. Those are odd words to describe a man you've agreed to join for dinner," her mother mused.

"That's the problem, Mom," Callen said, shoving a hand through the dark bangs that hung slightly in her eyes. "I don't know exactly how to describe him. He seemed so sad. And lonely."

"I see. So you want to make him happy and less lonely?"

"Is that so awful?"

Her mother slid an arm around her waist and hugged her slightly. "Not if you keep in mind that what you're offering Sam Longstreet is friendship. Just don't let yourself tumble head over heels in love with a man who's too wounded to love you back."

One

"I'm going to marry Sam Longstreet, and there's nothing you can do to stop me," Callen said to her father in a calm, brittle voice. Her brown eyes flashed with defiance. "What's wrong with Sam? He's a rancher, a close neighbor. Longstreet land has bordered Whitelaw land in northwest Texas for generations!"

Garth Whitelaw eyed his daughter, the youngest of his three grown children, with trepidation. She had been engaged twice, but never married. Both times, he had warned her she was making a mistake. Both times, she had disregarded his advice, only to break the engagements later when she learned the truth of what he had said. Now she was proposing a third prospective husband, this one as bad—maybe even worse—than the other two. Garth had learned that telling Callen no was like waving a red flag in front of a bull, but he felt so strongly that Sam was the wrong man for his daughter that he made his arguments anyway.

"Sam Longstreet will never amount to anything," he said. "He's a down-at-the-heels rogue with nothing to his name but a ramshackle ranch. At a guess, I'd say he's only interested in your money."

"That's despicable!" Callen retorted. "How can you even suggest such a thing?"

"Because it's true," Garth replied in a steely voice. "You're an heiress, Sam's a dirt-poor rancher. He was lucky to get through high school, and he hasn't done anything since to educate himself. He's a loner, and he's lazy. The Double L is falling down around him. What can the two of you possibly have in common?"

"Sam's a wonderful man," Callen argued. "He's just had a lot of hard luck lately. His father made some bad investments that took all their savings. I'll agree Sam has been reclusive in the months since his dad died, but that sort of blow would be hard on anyone who loved his father as much as Sam loved E.J."

Garth probably missed E. J. Longstreet as much or more than Sam did. The two older men had been good friends. It was a shame what had happened to E.J., and Garth sympathized with Sam's loss. But that didn't mean he wanted Sam for a son-in-law. He couldn't imagine what his daughter found attractive about the rancher. He asked again, "What do you see in him?"

Callen hesitated a moment before she replied. "Sam needs me, Daddy. And I need him. He makes me feel . . . special."

Garth snorted. "I'm not saying what happens between a man and woman between the sheets isn't important. But you're going to find it mighty tough sitting across from a lazy good-for-nothing at the breakfast table for the rest of your life."

Callen's lips flattened and her eyes narrowed. "I didn't mean Sam makes me feel special in bed. I meant— Oh, what's the use! I'm not going to change your mind, and you're not going to change mine. I wasn't asking your permission to marry Sam, I just wanted to let you know we're going to be married and invite you to the wedding."

"I won't be there," Garth said flatly.

Callen's chin quivered. She gritted her teeth to steady it before replying, "That's up to you, of course." She started for the front door of the ante-bellum-style mansion that had been built more than a century before as the main ranch house at Hawk's Way. She paused at the front door, waiting, hoping her father would change his mind. Her heart sank as she heard his parting words.

"If you marry Sam, you won't have a job here anymore." Garth knew the threat was a mistake the moment the words were out of his mouth, but it was too late to take them back. Callen was the best cutting horse trainer he had. She wouldn't have any trouble finding another job. And he didn't want to lose all contact with his only daughter. Though it had been years since he had said the words to her, he loved her dearly.

Callen's shoulders stiffened, then squared, before she turned to face her father. "I hope you'll change your mind, Daddy. Because come Friday, I'm going to be Mrs. Sam Longstreet."

Callen headed for the stable to saddle her horse. She needed some time alone to think. The canyons and gullies of Hawk's Way had long provided a haven, a ready balm for her soul. Once in the saddle, Callen aimed her horse into the Texas sun. It felt wonderful on her face, and the wind brushed her bangs away from her forehead and lifted her shoulder-length black hair so it flew in the breeze. She relaxed her jaw, which she realized was still clenched.

She was furious with her father for opposing her marriage to Sam and equally terrified that he might be right. He had been right twice before. But Sam was different, not at all like the previous two men she had planned to marry. In the first place, Sam was a rancher. She had grown up on Hawk's Way, and there wasn't anything she didn't know about cattle or cutting horses. She and Sam had that in common, since he had grown up on the Double L. But she would have been hard-pressed to name the specific things about Sam that made her so sure they were right for each other.

When she had gone to dinner with Sam three months ago, Callen had found herself utterly charmed by him. There was something dangerous about Sam, about his moods and the way he carried himself. And yet his eyes were so very sad. And kind. That was the word she would have used to describe his behavior toward her.

She could remember Sam's first kiss as though it had just happened. He had walked her to her car from the restaurant and stood there looking at her with eyes that spoke volumes. The closest light came from the restaurant, and they stood partly in shadow.

"You're beautiful," he said.

Callen had been told that before by more than one man, but Sam made her believe it. He cupped one cheek with his hand and brushed his callused thumb across her lips. She shivered at the touch. Her eyes had drifted closed as he slowly lowered his head.

His lips were incredibly soft as he pressed them to hers. He brushed them once, twice across her mouth before lifting his head to stare into her eyes once more.

He'd left her wanting much, much more.

It was only the first of many excursions together. They often went riding over Double L land and, if Callen were honest, she had to admit the place needed work. Fences were down, windmills screeched for want of oil, the barn needed some sideboards replaced and the house—at least from the outside—had seen much better days.

When she asked Sam about the rundown condition of the Double L, he had replied, "It takes money to make repairs. Not all of us are blessed with wealth."

Seeing how sensitive he was about the difference in their economic situations, she hadn't brought up the subject again.

Their second kiss had come a week after the first, at a moment when they had just stepped down to rest their horses. She was caught by surprise because it was a kiss of hunger, and she hadn't seen the need in Sam's eyes until he reached for her and pulled her into his embrace. His body was large and hard, and she had felt enveloped by him—safe, secure, and very much wanted. His hands moved hesitantly over her body at first, barely touching, reverently touching, and finally claiming her. She felt breathless when he finally released her.

"Sam . . . please." It was a plea to finish what he had started.

Sam shook his head and, in a voice harsh with need, said, "No, Callen. It wouldn't be right."

"Why not?"

He smiled ruefully. "In the first place, I don't have any kind of protection with me."

She blushed furiously. She should have thought of that herself.

"In the second place, you deserve better. A soft bed and a lover who belongs to you, heart and soul."

She hadn't known what to reply to that.

"Come on," he said, lifting her into the saddle. "We'd better get back to the house."

They had been seeing each other almost daily for a month when she asked if she could see the inside of his house.

Again, Sam shook his head no.

"Why not?" she demanded, fists perched on hips.

"Because I wouldn't trust myself alone with you if there was a bed anywhere nearby."

Callen had been flattered but was so used to getting her own way that she didn't give up. She pressed herself close to Sam, feeling the way his body tensed and hardened. "I wouldn't mind, Sam," she purred in her most seductive voice.

"I would," Sam said as he caught her by the arms and moved her away. "You deserve the best, Callen. You deserve to be treated with respect."

Callen met Sam's gaze, her eyes wide with surprise. His words were what every woman wanted to hear, yet her brow soon furrowed in confusion. His ideas concerning courtship were so...old-fashioned. He had to know, since she had been engaged twice, that she wasn't a virgin who needed to be protected from the importunities of a forceful male. But Sam had apparently put her on a pedestal. She found it awkward to stay balanced there, knowing herself to be far less than perfect. But, oh, how good it felt to be so cherished!

Then the precious moment had come, just two days ago, when Sam proposed to her.

"I know I'm not good enough for you," Sam began.

She pressed her fingertips to his lips. How could he not be good enough when he made her feel so wonderful?

"You deoorvc bettei," he insisted. "But I'll do my best to make your life as happy as I can. Will you marry me, Callen? Will you be my wife?"

Her throat was so tight with emotion that she hadn't been able to answer right away. At last she said, "Yes, Sam, I'll marry you. I want to be your wife."

He kissed her then, tenderly at first and then hungrily, his tongue sweeping into her mouth and claiming her. He hugged her so tightly she squeaked with pain. When he released her, they looked at each other and laughed with joy.

His eyes glittered in the sunlight, and for a moment she was frightened at their intensity. She shivered, and he pulled her close, murmuring, "Don't be frightened, Callen."

Until Sam spoke the words, she hadn't realized how scared she was. But the look in his eyes urged her to trust him. And she did. Sam would never hurt her the way she had been hurt before. He would never allow himself to be bought off by her father, as her first two lovers had done. Sam would only love her and respect her and protect her.

Was it any wonder she had fallen in love with him? Was it any wonder that, when he had proposed, she had said yes? Her father had suggested that Sam was another fortune hunter. That he was lazy and poor and just wanted to marry her for her money.

Callen didn't believe it. Sam loved her. She would stake her life on it. *Was* staking her life on it. Because, come Friday, she would be standing in front of a judge with Sam Longstreet by her side. And when the judge asked if she wanted to spend the rest of her life with Sam, she was going to say yes.

* * *

Sam Longstreet didn't want Callen's money, but neither was he marrying her for love. He had wooed her and won her with one specific purpose in mind: to get revenge on Garth Whitelaw.

Garth was the one who had convinced Sam's father, E.J., to invest his life savings in several ventures that had turned out to be swindles. Sam had been shocked to discover that Garth had led his father so far astray, since the two men had been friends for more years than anyone could count. His best friend's betrayal had made E.J. moody and morose. He had started drinking and rarely left the house.

Sam had tried to console his father when things were at their worst, but E.J. was inconsolable. After more than a hundred years, he would be the Longstreet who finally lost the Double L to creditors. Sam had come home from working on the range one day to find his father, whom he cherished, dead of a gunshot wound to the head.

He had nearly gone mad with grief.

He had sat for hours in the same room with his father's corpse, unable to move. The long hours he spent paralyzed had given him a lot of time to think. The more he thought about it, the more convinced he became that Garth Whitelaw had planned to dupe his father, knowing full well E.J. would lose his ranch. Then, when it went into foreclosure, Garth could buy the land for a pittance of its value and add it to Hawk's Way, thus replacing the several thousand acres Garth had given to his eldest son, Zach, on his twenty-first birthday. It was Garth Whitelaw's greedy desire to possess the Double L that was the direct cause of E. J. Longstreet's death.

On the day Sam buried his father, he confronted Garth at the graveyard with his knowledge of the other man's perfidy. He waited until Garth was alone and approached him.

"This is all your fault," he snarled. "E.J. followed your advice and lost everything he worked for all his life!"

"I never—"

"Don't try to deny it," Sam said in a savage voice. "My father never invested a penny until he talked to you. Only this time you told him what would serve your purposes. This time you led him into a swindle. You knew how he felt about the Double L. You ruined him. You killed him as surely as if you'd held the gun yourself!"

Garth blanched.

Before he could retort, his daughter, Callen, reached his side. She was wearing her long black hair in a ponytail, with a fringe of bangs that made her look surprisingly young. Sam remembered her as a bothersome kid always trailing along behind her older brothers, Zach and Falcon, not that he and her brothers had had much to do with each other then or now. He noted in a detached way that Callen had grown up to be quite a beauty.

Sam watched as Callen looked up with adoring eyes at her father. Then he caught Garth's unguarded look of love for his daughter. At that moment the idea had come to Sam that here was one sure way to get vengeance on his enemy. Garth had stolen his father; somehow he would take Garth's daughter from him.

As Garth walked away, Callen looked up at him. "I'm so sorry about your father."

Sam checked the retort that he didn't need any Whitelaw pity, and said, "Thanks."

His face remained a thing of carved granite as he stared down at her. It dawned on him how easily he could have his vengeance.

Sam knew about Callen's two previous engagements. He knew her father wouldn't think he was good enough for her. All he had to do was make her fall in love with him. Father and daughter were sure to argue, and it would split them apart. Then he would offer to marry her, force her to choose between him and her father. Either way, she would lose. And, therefore, Garth would lose. His vengeance would be all the sweeter when he told Callen—if she chose him instead of her father—why he had married her.

Sam hadn't wasted any time beginning his conquest of Callen. He wasn't without charm, he simply chose not to employ it most of the time. There, at his father's graveside, he let his gaze linger on Callen's lips and then focus on her eyes. They were a warm, tobacco brown.

She flushed prettily. "Is there anything I can do to help?"

"You can meet me for dinner in Amarillo," he said.

When he turned his gaze back to Garth at the graveside, he was pleased with the frown he saw on the other man's face. He knew Garth wanted to warn him to keep his distance from Callen, but the older man kept his lips pressed tight as he whirled abruptly and walked away.

When all the other mourners were gone and Sam was finally alone in the tiny graveyard that held the mortal remains of generations of Longstreets, he stood near the cold headstone that marked his father's final resting place and made a solemn vow to avenge his death.

"I promise you, Dad, however long it takes, no matter what I have to do, Garth Whitelaw is going to suffer for what he did to you."

His courtship of Callen had been accomplished with surprising speed. He suspected she had felt sorry for him at first, and thus her barriers were all down.

He had swept her off her feet with honeyed words and a few searing kisses. He hadn't bedded her, using old-fashioned morals as an excuse. His charade of respect and caring had worked even better than he had hoped. Within weeks she had fallen in love with him. When he proposed, she had accepted with tears of joy in her eyes.

The best part had been when Garth Whitelaw came to the Double L with his checkbook open, asking how much Sam wanted to call off the wedding.

"I don't want your money, Whitelaw." Sam hadn't been able to keep from smiling. Garth was a fool to think he was going to be able to pay for his guilt with cash.

"I know you need money to keep the Double L from foreclosure. Tell me how much, and I'll loan it to you interest free," Garth offered.

"I don't want or need your help," he retorted. Truthfully, he was surprised that Garth had tried to buy him off with that particular offer. Sam figured the man must have had some other plan in mind to put the Double L in his debt. He wasn't going to fall for it.

"I want you to stay away from Callen," Garth said.

"She's a grown woman. She can make her own decisions."

"She's made her share of bad ones."

"And I'm a bad one?"

"The worst."

"Does Callen know you're here?"

Garth shifted restlessly, uneasily. "No."

A wicked grin split Sam's face as he relished Garth's discomfort. "Don't worry. I won't tell her you tried to buy me off."

Garth hadn't bothered thanking him, just stalked down the rickety stairs that led from Sam's sagging front porch, gunning the engine of his pickup as he headed down the dusty road.

So far, Callen had remained firm in the face of her family's disapproval. Sam had to admire her for that. He fought back the nagging conscience that told him it was wrong to hurt an innocent woman for the transgressions of her father. He was only doing what was necessary to avenge the wrong done to E.J. Garth Whitelaw hadn't given a thought to Sam's pain when he had ruined Sam's father. He quieted his conscience with the thought that when it was all over, Callen would still be alive. E.J. was gone forever.

The wedding was tomorrow. He wondered if Garth would find some way to stop it. He hoped the older man tried. It would surely put a wide breach between Garth and his daughter. It was a breach Sam intended to extend until father and daughter were totally alienated.

Sam swallowed the bitter bile that rose in his throat when he thought of the senselessness of his father's death. He needed the marriage to Callen to achieve his revenge against her father. It was important to guard against feeling anything for her. He had to bear in mind that Callen Whitelaw was just a tool he was using to achieve his goal of revenge. He had to forget about the softness of her skin, the sweetness of her kisses, the look of adoration and trust in her eyes.

Sam's lips pressed flat. When it came time to say his vows before the judge, he would do it. And crush the conscience that urged him to let the girl go free.

Two

Callen came alone to the county courthouse for her wedding. Her father had held fast to his vow to be absent, and her mother had refused to side against her father. Her brother, Falcon, couldn't leave Dallas because his wife, Mara, was pregnant and near term, and her brother, Zach, had told her plainly that she was making the worst mistake of her life, and he wasn't going to be a part of it. In a privileged existence that had been marked by periods of loneliness, Callen had never felt so alone.

As she paced the hardwood floor in front of the judge's chambers dressed in an antique lace dress, wearing an ivory felt cloche and carrying a pungent bouquet of gardenias, Callen wondered whether she was playing the fool. Was her family right? Was Sam actually a fortune hunter?

Callen glanced at her watch. Sam was late. For a half second she wondered whether he might not show up at all. Before that thought could take root, she saw him come through the imposing double doors of the courthouse. As glad as she was to see him, Callen couldn't help the feeling of foreboding that wedged in her throat and made it difficult to speak.

Sam walked right up to her, reached for her hands and took them in his. "You look beautiful," he murmured.

Unfortunately there was no way Callen could honestly return the compliment. In fact, she was sorely disappointed by Sam's appearance. "You didn't dress up."

Sam flushed. "No."

No excuse, no explanation, just no. His sun-bleached hair was shaggy and needed a cut, nor had he shaved for at least a day. His boots were worn, and his jeans were frayed. He looked like he hadn't slept for a week, and if he had, he'd done it in his clothes. The sun-lined face that had become so dear to her was carved in granite. And his green eyes, the kind, tender eyes that had made her fall in love with him, looked as hard as cut glass.

Callen shivered. Sam seemed a stranger. This was a side of him she had never seen. He was the saddle tramp Zach had named him, shady and disreputable. Two spots of heat rose on her cheeks when she thought of the scathing comments her father would have made if he had seen her bridegroom looking like this. Callen was ashamed and embarrassed by Sam's appearance. The thought flashed across her mind that she ought to run like hell from Sam, from this marriage.

She couldn't look at Sam, afraid he would see what was in her thoughts. Appearances shouldn't matter, she told herself. She had known Sam was poor. She had seen him unshaven in the past, in fact, had seen him in the same Western shirt and jeans he was wearing now. But that didn't ease her worry. She had expected Sam to treat their marriage, the ceremony at least, with the same reverence she felt. After all, they were beginning a new life together. If anything, Sam's appearance evidenced contempt for the ritual of marriage. Obviously she had mistaken his feelings on the subject.

What else are you mistaken about, Callen?

Callen fought back the voices of her father and her brother, both of whom had warned her not to marry Sam. She opened her mouth to tell Sam she couldn't go through with it and shut it again. She couldn't be wrong about Sam. She refused to be wrong about

Sam. There must be some good reason why he hadn't taken the time to improve his appearance, an emergency on the ranch or some other disaster.

"Was there some trouble on the ranch this morning?" she asked.

"No."

"No cattle stampede? Brush fire? Pack of howling wolves at the door?" she teased.

"No."

She pursed her lips ruefully. "You overslept?"

"No."

She couldn't think of another reason that would explain Sam's careless appearance . . . and he wasn't offering one. She looked up into his green eyes, which softened slightly as he stared down at her, and waited for an explanation.

"I went to visit my father's grave," he said at last.

"Oh." Her shoulders relaxed. Of course. He was still grieving. He must have stayed at the small, fenced plot too long, and then not had time to remedy his appearance. Now that she examined Sam's face more closely, she saw red-rimmed eyes, a clenched jaw. Yes, he was definitely still grieving. It must be awful to know his father hadn't lived to see his only son marry, hadn't lived to know his grandchildren.

The thought of producing grandchildren brought a rosy glow to Callen's cheeks. She had thought a lot about what it would be like to lie with Sam, to grow large with his child, to hold a baby in her arms and have Sam smile at her, as they admired their child together.

Callen reminded herself of everything she had learned about Sam over the past three months. He was kind. He was considerate. He was charming. He was even handsome in a rugged sort of way. And his eyes made her feel cherished and loved. Or at least they had. Perhaps it was the memory of his father, the grief and the sadness, that had stolen the warmth from his eyes and made him look so harsh and hard when she had first seen him today.

She loved Sam for who he was, not for the outer trappings of the man, not for his wealth—or lack of it—but for the way he made her feel. She squeezed Sam's hands, raised her eyes to meet his and offered him a tremulous smile. "Come on, Sam. The judge is waiting."

"Your family?"

She swallowed over the lump in her throat. "They're not coming."

"Then it's just us?"

Callen nodded. Sam's lips pressed flat and his eyes narrowed. For an instant she wanted to flee, to save herself from Sam, from the possibility of a failed marriage. But it would be devastating to break a *third* engagement. She wouldn't be able to look her father in the eye. It was too late to back out now.

Callen took comfort in the thought that she knew Sam better than her father did. Sam would never hurt her. And if he did, her father would never hear of it from her. She would do whatever was necessary to make the marriage a good one. As one of the Three Whitelaw Brats, and with a lifetime of outmaneuvering and outsmarting two older brothers to her credit, she had developed the ability to rescue herself from the toughest situations. She loved Sam. Somehow, this was all going to work out.

She looked up at Sam, her heart in her eyes. There was a flash of some strong emotion on his face before he kissed her with a combination of tenderness and fierceness that left her breathless. The thought came to her, powerful and overwhelming. *I want to spend my life with this man.*

"Come on," Sam grated in a husky voice. "Let's go."

Sam felt like sobbing with relief—and disgust. He had done what he could to keep Callen Whitelaw from walking into disaster, but she hadn't backed away in time to save either of them. He led her toward the judge's chambers. It was time to take the next step on his trail of vengeance.

His eyes were red-rimmed because he hadn't slept. His conscience had smote him the day before the wedding, demanding that he free Callen from the devil's bargain he was about to make with her. He had tried desperately to think of a way to take his vengeance on Garth Whitelaw directly, without involving his daughter. But he couldn't think of anything that was as likely to cause Garth the same pain he endured himself as stealing someone he loved away from him.

In endeavoring to free Callen from the morass into which he had drawn her, Sam made a stunning discovery. He wanted her. Somehow during the course of winning her admiration, he had come to admire her, as well. She had a wicked sense of humor, a smile that flashed often enough to lift even his leadened heart, skin softer than silk, and lips as sweet as anything he had ever tasted. His groin tightened at the mere thought of bedding her. He suspected his desire for her had contributed to his inability to come up with another route of vengeance.

By the same token, because he had allowed Callen to get under his skin, it was going to be difficult to hurt her, as he must if he was going to achieve his goal of hurting her father. In the early hours of the morning, wretchedly alone, with the grief of his father's death making his stomach spin and his chest ache, he had come up with the idea of presenting himself to Callen in such a state of disarray that she would be the one to back away from him. He couldn't push her away; she was going to have to leave him of her own accord.

It hadn't worked.

Callen's family had sheltered her from the harsher facts of life, and with the confidence of the innocent, she had simply looked past the facade he had erected to shove her away and embraced the man she found beyond it. He sighed inwardly, damning her for making him want her even more, damning himself for being bastard enough to go through with his plan.

They had reached the door to the judge's chamber when Callen's eldest brother showed up. Sam eyed Zach warily, aware of the animosity on the other man's face.

Callen appeared delighted by Zach's arrival. "Zach! You came!" She let go of Sam's hand and flung herself into her brother's open arms.

Sam met Zach's narrowed eyes over Callen's head and knew the other man would do whatever he could to stop the wedding. Sam welcomed the coming fight with relish. He had wanted—needed—to hit out at the injustice of his father's death. With Garth unavailable, Zach Whitelaw made a very satisfying target.

"I'm so glad you changed your mind and decided to come," Callen said with breathless excitement. "I would have gone through with the wedding even if no one from the family came, but I'm so glad to have someone to stand beside me."

"I'm not here to support you," Zach said in a hard voice.

Callen stepped back, aware suddenly of the hostility that bristled between her tall, intimidating brother and the lean, dangerous man who would soon be her husband. Her heart sank. There was no way the two of them were going to be reconciled in the few minutes she had before the wedding. If it came to a choice, Callen knew she would go with Sam. That would surely make Zach even angrier.

Callen stared up at her brother. "Why did you come, Zach?"

Zach's eyes were on Sam. "To tell the sonofabitch you're getting set to marry that if he lays one hand on you, if he hurts you in any way, he'll have to answer to me."

Callen heard Sam's hiss as he took an outraged breath, felt his body stiffen, saw his stance widen for battle. She put herself between the two men, laying one hand on Zach's chest and the other on Sam's to keep them from coming to blows. "Please," she said. "Don't fight."

When she turned to Zach, she found no sympathy in his dark eyes, only scorn and anger.

"You're a fool to be marrying beneath yourself like this," Zach raged. "Take a good look at him, Callen. He's a disgrace."

When Callen didn't immediately turn back to Sam, her brother put a strong hand on her chin and forced her face around toward her bridegroom. Callen shook herself free as she heard Sam's growl of challenge.

"Let her go!"

"She's my sister. I'll do as I please."

"She belongs to me now," Sam retorted. "You damn well better leave her alone."

"The hell I will!"

"Stop it! Both of you!" Callen cried, shoving against two hard, heaving chests with the flat of her hands.

Zach continued his scorching castigation of her bridegroom without even taking a breath. His dark eyes burned as he held her gaze. "Think about who you're going to marry," he said ruthlessly. "Sam Longstreet barely made it through high school. He's got no dreams, no goals. Hell, all he wants is your money! He'll embarrass you in front of company because he looks like hell warmed over most of the time. Like now," he said, nodding with his chin toward Sam. "Is that the way a bridegroom ought to dress for his wedding?"

Callen looked, then lowered her eyes. She had been willing to disregard Sam's appearance, to excuse it. That was difficult with Zach standing beside her pointing out Sam's faults. She felt a flush of embarrassment, then a burning resentment toward her brother and, to a lesser extent, toward Sam for putting her in the position of having to defend something she had condemned herself.

"What Sam's wearing doesn't matter to me," she said stubbornly.

Zach grabbed her by the shoulders and turned her so she was facing him again. Her hand dropped away from Sam's chest, but she was aware of him standing behind her, of the leashed tension that sizzled and threatened violence.

Then Zach was speaking, his face so close she could see the temper smoldering in his dark eyes. "The man doesn't have any friends. You'll be all alone once you're living with him at the Double L," he warned. "Don't marry him, Callen. Put an end to this nonsense."

"I love him," Callen said in a quiet voice.

Zach pulled her into a protective embrace, almost crushing her with his strength. "God, Callen, what can I do to make you change your mind?"

"Nothing. I'm going to marry Sam, with or without your approval ... or Daddy's blessing."

Zach's next words were spoken low in her ear so there was no possibility of Sam overhearing. "When you decide to leave him, when you recognize your mistake, you'll be welcome at my place."

He levered her away and into Sam's waiting arms. "Don't forget what I said, Longstreet. You harm one hair on her head, and I'll come after you." Then he stalked past Sam and out the courthouse door.

Callen stood there with Sam's arms wrapped comfortingly around her, hard-pressed to hold back the tears that threatened. The third time around she certainly hadn't planned on a lavish wedding. But she would have liked some of her family to be there, and she would have liked her groom to be a little better dressed.

She raised her blurred gaze to Sam's face and saw a flash of sympathy in his green eyes that disappeared so quickly she wasn't sure it had been there in the first place.

"Do you still want to marry me?" Sam asked in a taunting voice. "Or has your brother talked you out of it?"

Sam was giving her one last chance to back out, Callen realized. She searched his eyes for any sign of the affection he had shown her during their courtship. It seemed strangely absent. She felt frightened.

What if her family was right, and she was wrong? She couldn't afford to make another mistake. But neither could she face the humiliation of crawling back home with her tail between her legs.

Stubborn pride kept Callen standing at Sam's side. She wasn't going to let her family talk her out of something she knew was right. Her relationship with Sam over the past three months had revealed the source of a vague discontent she had felt for years. She was thirty-two years old. She had yearned for someone to love, someone to love her. She wanted children, several of them, and she wasn't getting any younger. And she needed a home of her own, a place where she belonged. Sam had promised to fulfill those needs.

Furthermore, Sam had been a neighbor for years. If he had really been a fortune hunter, wouldn't he have come courting a lot sooner? He couldn't possibly have the sinister motives for marriage that her father and brother had suggested he did.

"Let's go on in." Sam put a hand to the small of her back and ushered her inside the judge's chambers. She wasn't acquainted with the judge, nor with the secretary and bailiff he offered as witnesses.

Callen heard nothing the judge said as he began the words of the ceremony. She was too caught up in remembering her family's accusations against Sam and her own reservations about what she was doing.

"For richer or poorer, in sickness and in health..."

He's a fortune hunter! He's only after your money!

Callen closed her eyes as a wave of nausea rolled over her. It was terrifying to defy her father, terrifying to ignore the warning signs that were all around her and follow her heart.

I love him.

That was the response that had silenced her father. That was the response that had silenced Zach. But was her love enough?

"Do you have a ring?" the judge asked.

Sam added a simple band of white gold to the diamond engagement ring he had given her that had belonged to his mother.

Then it was her turn. She knew how much a rancher worked with his hands. A ring that wasn't simple would be a nuisance and likely wouldn't be worn. So she had bought him a plain gold band. She saw the flicker of surprise in his eyes and then what looked like pleasure as she slipped it on his finger.

The ceremony was over too quickly. The judge smiled at them and said, "You may kiss the bride."

Callen was ready for a quick peck on the lips. But Sam pulled her slowly toward him until their bodies were aligned and then lowered his mouth to claim hers. The kiss was thorough, and before he was done they were both breathing hard.

When she turned an eye back to the judge, his grin had broadened. He reached out to shake Sam's hand. "It's always a pleasure to see two people in love."

Callen noticed the smile on Sam's lips, but it never reached his eyes. Was it the mention of the word *love* that bothered him? Sam had never said the words to her, but he had shown her in a dozen different ways that he cherished her. Besides, she thought with a rueful smile, this was no time to be having second thoughts. The deed was done. She was Mrs. Sam Longstreet.

Sam was no longer smiling by the time they reached the steps outside the courthouse door. "Do you want to drive to the house together, or follow me in your car?"

"Do you have a preference?" She wanted him to say that he couldn't bear for her to be separated from him for a moment. She wanted to be romanced on her wedding day. Sam's response was too practical for her peace of mind.

"We'd only have to make another trip back for your car," he said. "Go ahead and follow me to the house." He turned his back on her and headed for his pickup, leaving her standing alone on the court-house steps.

Callen noticed he hadn't called it a home.

She tried not to feel abandoned, tried to put the best possible face on the situation. But this wasn't what she had imagined. What had happened to the romantic swain who had swept her off her feet?

Callen pursed her lips thoughtfully. If she didn't stop seeing trouble everywhere, she was going to drive herself crazy. Things would work out. She only had to remember that she loved Sam. And he loved her, whether he said the words or not. She was married to Sam, for better or worse.

Unfortunately, when Sam carried her over the threshold of the Double L ranch house, she saw how bad *worse* could be.

Her father's description of Sam's place as a "ramshackle ranch" was very much on the mark, Callen realized. She had known the wood frame structure with its tin roof was old. But she wasn't prepared for what she found inside when Sam set her back on her feet after carrying her over the threshold.

"Well? What do you think?"

Callen searched for something nice to say. "It's...clean." Perhaps neat was a better word than clean. She eyed the dust that had gathered on every surface, the cobwebs in the corners. What furniture the house contained—and it was decorated Spartanly—was old and rat-bitten. There were no antiques here that had been lovingly polished to a high sheen like there were at Hawk's Way. Just second-hand junk.

No wonder Sam hadn't wanted to bring her into the house. There was nothing here that could be admired. Until this moment, Callen hadn't realized how luxurious her life-style at Hawk's Way had been, or how spoiled she had been by the comforts she had always taken for granted.

The condition of the furniture, of the house itself, suggested things had been going downhill at the Double L for far longer than the three months since E.J. had died. The place reeked of ongoing impoverishment.

Her father's words echoed in her head. *He's only interested in you for your money.* She shoved them back out again.

"It needs a little work," she said with a hard-won smile. "But I'm more than willing to supply the elbow grease." She walked around the combination parlor and office excitedly pointing out the improvements she would make.

"First thing is to buy you a new desk. Then, a sofa placed just so in front of the fireplace, a couple of leather chairs—something comfortable with an ottoman for you—a few tables, lamps, some art for the walls, a carpet on the floor, and I guarantee you won't recognize the place."

"All those things cost money," Sam said.

Her smile broadened. "I'm rich. I can afford it."

He shook his head.

Callen felt a well of joy. *He didn't want her money!* Her father was wrong. She was moving toward Sam when his next words stopped her.

"We'll need that money to make back payments on the mortgage and to pay debts I've accumulated. I doubt there'll be much left for frivolities like furniture and rugs."

"What?" Callen was staring at Sam as though she had never seen him before. "I have plenty of money—"

He cut her off with a harsh oath. "It's not enough. I have a fairly good idea of the extent of your fortune. I'm telling you, it'll be eaten up by the cost of keeping possession of the Double L."

"Then we'll sell this place and—"

"No, Callen. This is my home—your home now. We're staying come hail or high water." In response to the shocked look on her face, he said, "Surely your father mentioned I was in financial trouble." His mouth twisted cynically. "You must have known how bad things are. The condition of the outbuildings, the fences that needed mending, the rundown condition of the house. You couldn't have been blind to all of it."

"I...wasn't...exactly." Only she had worn blinders, refusing to see reality, lost in a fog of euphoria: a fool in love. In one respect—Sam's need for her money—her father had been absolutely right. But she wasn't going to cry craven and run. She loved Sam. And if he needed her money, he was welcome to it.

Callen lifted her chin. "Whatever money you need, you're welcome to spend. Use it how you think best."

Sam's eyes narrowed. He was astonished at Callen's generous offer. He had expected trouble when he told her he wanted to invest her fortune in the Double L. With the marriage still unconsummated, it was a sure way of goading her to run, to save herself from the fate he had planned for her. But her brown eyes had flared with a militant light and that stubborn chin of hers had bucked up. And she had offered him everything she had.

He refused to feel guilt or remorse, even though the pull of both made the skin stretch taut across his cheekbones. She had made a free choice to be his wife. She had stayed when she saw how rough things were going to be. Well, so be it. He had committed himself. It was time to get on with his revenge.

Three

___

"Come here, Callen."

Callen saw the fierce desire in Sam's eyes and felt an answering desire rise within her. Now that the moment was at hand, however, she was uncertain what to do. "It's broad daylight," she said with a shy smile.

"I want to see you when I make love to you for the first time," Sam replied.

A rush of pleasure and embarrassment painted Callen's cheeks a vivid rose. "There's not much to see," she murmured. Her breasts weren't anything to shout about, and while she had a narrow waist and a decent pair of legs, she was closer to cute than pretty, closer to pretty than beautiful. It would have been easier to do this the first time in the dark.

"Callen."

The single word was a command that compelled her to obey. She took the several steps that brought her near enough for Sam to reach out and pull her close. His arms folded around her possessively.

Callen felt safe, secure, treasured. Those weren't the feelings she had expected and, as it turned out, weren't the feelings she experienced moments later when Sam's mouth came down to capture hers.

Hungry. Unbridled. Ruthless. Sam demanded total surrender, and Callen was helpless to resist. The blood raced in her veins, sending heat and shuddering sensation throughout her body. Now Callen understood why Sam had kept his desire under control in the past. She was overwhelmed by feelings she had never imagined. His effect on her was devastating.

"Sam," she gasped. She clung to him, breathless and almost dizzy. She was shivering and couldn't seem to stop.

"Callen," he breathed in her ear. It was a plea. It was a promise.

He lifted her into his arms and carried her into his bedroom. It was darker there because heavy curtains covered the windows. She clung to Sam's shoulders as he leaned over and pulled down the covers on the bed, barely toeing off her shoes before he laid her down. She noticed the bed was made with fresh white sheets that had been tucked in with almost military precision. He had known he would bring her here. He had cared what she would think—about this, at least.

The sheets were cool, or maybe it was simply that she was so warm in contrast. He stood above her, his green eyes lit with a fierce, primitive light.

"Take off your clothes," he said.

Callen was caught unawares. She had expected him to do that for her, had anticipated it, in fact. He stood above her, arms akimbo, legs widespread, with that devouring look on his face, and waited.

She sat up and turned her back to him before lifting her hair out of the way. "Can you get these few buttons for me?" It seemed like an eternity before she felt the brush of his hands against her nape. She felt the sweep of air as her back was exposed and a moment later the touch of his mouth against her skin. A shiver of delight ran down her spine.

When he was nearly finished, Sam slid onto the bed behind her. His hands slipped around to cup her breasts. She felt him exhale slowly as his hands shaped and molded the small mounds.

"You feel so good."

The sound of his voice rasped in her ear, sending another shiver through her. Her hands dropped to rest on his as she leaned her head back against his shoulder. "I've dreamed about this so often...."

"So have I," he confessed. "You feel so good, so right in my hands."

"There's not much there," she said with a wry smile.

"Enough. Plenty," he said as he turned her in his arms.

She gasped as his mouth latched onto one breast through the lace. She felt the nip of his teeth and laughed breathlessly. "Maybe I ought to finish taking this off."

He lifted his head and released her. "All right. Go ahead."

She was suddenly shy again. The unbuttoned dress slid off her shoulders, revealing the white silk camisole she wore. She rose on her knees and shoved the dress and a half-slip down, then sat and pulled them off over her bare legs. She hadn't worn nylons in deference to the June heat, so she was left in nothing but her silk tap pants and camisole.

She started to lower the straps of her camisole, but Sam reached out a hand to stop her. She followed his eyes downward and saw that her nipples had peaked beneath the silk. There was a damp spot near her right breast where his mouth had been. He lowered his head and suckled her through the cloth.

Callen groaned. She had never felt anything so exquisite. Her hands slid into Sam's hair, which was thick and silky to the touch, while her head arched backward in ecstasy.

Sam took his time removing the rest of her clothing. It was difficult for Callen to lie still under his sharp gaze once he had her bare.

"You're beautiful, Callen."

In that moment she believed she was beautiful, despite her too small breasts and her straight black hair that refused to hold a curl and the spattering of freckles across her nose.

"I want to see you," she said, reaching up for the first of the buttons on his shirt. She had three unbuttoned when his patience deserted him. Callen laughed as Sam tore off his shirt, yanked off his boots and socks and reached for his belt buckle. He was naked moments later, and the laugh caught in her throat.

Whatever faults Sam might have had, his body wasn't one of them. Callen let her eyes roam from broad shoulders and muscled arms, down a chest that was furred with dark hair, past a washboard belly, to the curls that surrounded his arousal. His legs were long, his thighs sinewy and taut.

"You're the one who's beautiful," she managed to say.

He smiled.

Oh, what a wonderful smile it was! His white teeth flashed, and his eyes crinkled at the corners. She felt warm all over. Then came the laugh, up from his belly, past his chest and out of his mouth, a full, rich, happy sound.

She grinned. "What's so funny?"

"You thinking I'm beautiful."

"But you are," she insisted.

He snorted, a male sound of dismissal. "You're the special one, Callen." He sat on the bed beside her and let his callused fingertips stroke across her belly. "I can't believe you're mine."

Callen felt revered, cherished. She had done the right thing marrying Sam. She hadn't made a mistake. Sam couldn't touch her like this, hold her in his arms, stroke her mouth with his tongue in just that way if he didn't care for her.

He took his time loving her. His eyes constantly roamed her body, following where he touched. When he joined their bodies, making them one, he watched that, too. She had never been so aware of herself as a woman, never been so aware of the aching need to give everything she had to another human being.

Callen heard Sam's groan of agony and pleasure in the moment he thrust inside her, felt her muscles contract to hold him there. His hands lifted her buttocks as he made sweet, sweet love to her. She touched him everywhere she could reach, returning the caresses he had so freely given her. In her ultimate joy, she grasped his hair and pulled his mouth down to join hers as they cried out in exultation.

Afterward, she lay sated in his arms, breathless, her chest heaving. Their bodies were sweat-slick in the heat, and she realized suddenly that the house wasn't air-conditioned, that it was the breeze flowing from behind the curtains through the open windows that cooled their bodies. No wonder the curtains had been drawn, she thought. It kept out the hot sun. It was one more indication of the *worse* to go with the *better* in this marriage.

Right at this moment, Callen didn't have any complaints. She stretched lazily and felt Sam's hand slide down her thigh. It felt good, warm and rough against her skin. Sam was, quite simply, an incredible lover. She shouldn't have been surprised, but she was. She hadn't thought of him as the sort of man who dated a lot. So where had he learned to be so knowledgeable of a woman's needs in bed?

The answer to that question was easy, once Callen thought about it, though thinking at all was difficult with Sam's hand caressing her. A man as kind and considerate as Sam Longstreet would naturally be a good lover, because he would always be concerned about the other person's pleasure. She decided he deserved some thanks for his thoughtfulness. So she slid her hand along his naked flank, returning the caresses he bestowed upon her. She could feel the strength, the sinew and muscle that surrounded bone. She gave a little shove, and he rolled over onto his back.

"What's this?" he asked.

"I'm going to have my wicked way with you," Callen answered.

"By all means." His grin was far more wicked than anything she could have imagined doing to him. He lay still beneath her hands. Actually, not quite still. His body undulated beneath her onslaught, until he rolled her over beneath him and took up where she had left off.

They didn't leave the bed all day. It was full dark before either of them thought of anything except the delights to be found in the other's body. It was Sam's stomach that finally protested with a loud growl.

"I'm hungry," he admitted.

Callen snuggled closer. "Me, too."

"Who's going to get out of bed and fix supper?"

"I suppose I ought to," Callen said with a huge yawn.

"You're exhausted."

Callen heard the surprise and remorse in Sam's voice. She smiled to herself. "I hope you keep me this tired all the time," she teased.

She felt his body relax and heard his chuckle. "I might have gone a little crazy. I just never thought—"

He cut himself off and abruptly rose so that her hair, which was caught under his shoulder, got yanked hard enough to hurt. She cried out, then heard him swear as he stubbed his toe on the bedstead.

"Are you all right?" he called. Then, "Where the hell is the lamp?"

"I suspect it's where it's always been." Callen restrained a giggle as she reached out and snapped on a lamp beside the bed. She squinted her eyes until they adjusted to the light. When she could open them without pain, she saw that Sam was staring fixedly at her. She looked down and found there were small love bruises on her body where he had staked his claim. Her breasts were still flushed and rosy from their latest round of lovemaking. She quickly grappled for the sheet to cover herself.

"Don't. I..." He swallowed hard. "I like looking at you."

She forced herself to lie still. It was plain he wanted her again.

Fortunately—or unfortunately—his stomach chose that moment to growl again. He grabbed his jeans and stepped into them before heading for the kitchen in a hurry. "Stay where you are. I'll get us something to eat."

The first thing she did was jump out of bed and race for the standing oval mirror in the corner to see for herself how she looked. *Good Lord!* she thought. *That's what he finds attractive?*

Her hair was tangled beyond combing, her breasts were the same tiny size they'd always been, and she hadn't grown any taller. But a second look revealed the dreamy glow in her dark brown eyes, the heat beneath her skin that made her complexion pink and rosy, and the puffy softness of her lips where she had been thoroughly kissed. She looked like a woman who had spent most of the day making love with a man she adored.

She heard Sam returning, and scurried back to bed. Well, why not? If the man wanted to wait on her, who was she to complain? She was sitting up in bed when he entered the room, but she had chickened out and pulled the sheet up under her arms. There was such a thing as modesty, after all. She hadn't become a total wanton in one day. Had she? One glance at Sam's face, and she was afraid she had. She let the sheet fall and heard him gasp. He set the tray of soup and sandwiches on a dry sink across the room and came to her without another word.

The supper he had prepared sat forgotten.

When Sam woke, he felt disoriented. It took him a moment to realize the heat he felt came from another body snuggled up close. He eased himself away from Callen—from his wife—and sat up on the edge of the bed letting his eyes become accustomed to the dark. He wondered what time it was and sought out the alarm he kept next to his bed. The digital clock told him it was barely 10:00 p.m. It seemed much later.

He felt exhausted, but at the same time more rested than he had at any time since his father's death. He had reason to feel relaxed. His plan for vengeance had well and truly begun. He had taken the first steps to attach his wife's affections. Before he could take Callen away from her father, he had to be sure that if she was forced to choose, she would choose him. He had to be sure she was well and truly in love.

So he had made love to her as though she were the most precious of women. He had given her all of himself—or almost all. He hadn't given her his heart. He didn't love her. That would be a disaster and ruin his carefully laid plans. But he had created the illusion of love to the best of his ability.

It was only after that first incredibly powerful climax that he had realized the danger to himself. Yet he hadn't been able to deny himself the opportunity of making love to her again. She was all satiny softness and fiery desire. He hadn't been able to resist coming back for more. And more. He hadn't known he could want a woman like he wanted Callen. He was going to have to be careful. He had to remember at all times that his real purpose in marrying her was to cause her father pain.

Callen stretched and her foot reached out and stroked his thigh. "Come back to bed, Sam," she murmured.

He ought to get up and leave her now. He could feel the loose ropes binding him to her, even as he sought to bind her to himself. But he was the one in control. He could escape the noose whenever he chose, or use whatever means were necessary to cut himself free when the time came. He surrendered to the call and joined Callen in bed.

The next time he woke, it was dawn. Lately, because he couldn't sleep at night, he had dropped into bed exhausted at sunrise. But he had a mission this morning that had him out of bed the instant he realized what time it was. He had to make it to town, to the Stanton Hotel Café, where all the ranchers gathered early to drink coffee and listen to the stock and grain prices on the radio and compare notes before beginning the day. Garth Whitelaw would be there. And Sam had a few things to say to his new father-in-law.

The hotel had been built in the 1880s, and it still featured several of the original Victorian sofas in the lobby along with a Turkish carpet and some silvered mirrors in elaborate mahogany frames. The hotel café dated from the 1950s. It had a long service bar with stools that had red plastic seats and chrome backs. Someone had added trophy deer antlers on the walls, along with macramé wall hangings from the 1970s and a few pictures of the hotel when it had been in its prime.

Sam saw four ranchers at the far end of the bar. They sat in the same seats every morning. Garth Whitelaw was sitting on the stool closest to him, near the center of the bar. The stool next to Garth was empty, and Sam slid onto it.

He stared straight ahead, looking into the mirror behind the bar. He could see the faces of everyone reflected there. Sam noticed that he looked more than a little the worse for wear. He was wearing a hat that hid most of his hair, but it obviously needed a cut. He hadn't shaved and, to his chagrin, there was a love bruise under his right ear that Garth Whitelaw couldn't miss. Sam braced his elbows on the bar and ordered himself a cup of coffee from the waitress and proprietor of the café, Ida Mae Cooper.

The conversation at the bar had stopped. He let his eyes slide over three of the ranchers, daring any one of them to say anything. They each found something of interest to occupy themselves and avoided meeting his glance. When his green eyes met Garth's stony gray ones, he let his contempt show on his face.

"Offering some more good advice this morning?" Sam taunted. "You men might want to take what Garth Whitelaw says with a grain of salt. He tends to change the truth to fit his purpose."

There was an ominous silence as the men at the bar absorbed the insult.

Garth stiffened. He set down his cup of coffee and turned to Sam. "Are you calling me a liar?"

"If the shoe fits..."

Ida Mae sloshed some coffee into Garth's cup. "Don't want no fightin' in here, boys." Nobody could remember when Ida Mae hadn't been running the coffee shop. She had grown up on a ranch in the area, so she knew how to handle a rowdy crowd. Not that things got rowdy much these days. Only, Ida Mae could see that Sam had coming looking for trouble, and she knew for a fact that Garth was more than willing to give it to him.

"Why aren't you home with your wife?" Garth demanded.

A sneer cut across Sam's face. "I left her asleep in bed. She was plumb wore out."

"That's no way to talk about my daughter," Garth warned. "Or your wife, for that matter."

Sam was too intent on hurting Garth to care that he was acting in a manner that was totally alien to him. He would have killed any other man who spoke such a slur against his wife. But Callen wasn't just his wife, she was also Garth Whitelaw's daughter. She was part and parcel of his revenge. He was here to hurt Garth Whitelaw, not to protect his wife's name.

"I just thought you'd like to know I'll be going to the bank today to take care of my back mortgage payments," he said.

Garth's eyes narrowed.

"Can you believe it? Callen offered me her fortune," Sam said with a snide grin intended to raise the hair on Garth's neck.

"Why, you—" Garth started to rise, but was stopped by Sam's wagging finger.

"Uh-uh," Sam cautioned. "Ida Mae wouldn't like it if you messed up her place." He leaned closer and said in a voice not intended to be heard by the other men, "The Double L is lost to you, Whitelaw. Soon, your daughter will be, too."

"What the hell do you mean by that?" Garth shot back.

"Just remember what I said, Whitelaw." He rose, and Garth reached out to grab his arm. He yanked it free. "Stay away from me and my wife, do you hear?"

"I'll see my daughter—"

"She's not your daughter anymore," Sam said. "She's *my* wife. Stay away from the Double L, and leave Callen alone."

"If this is about E.J.—"

"You're damn straight it's about E.J.," Sam said, his face contorted in fury. "I want you to know what it feels like to lose someone you love and know they're gone forever."

"What the hell is wrong with you?" Garth demanded. "I had nothing to do with E.J.'s death."

"Nothing anyone can prove," Sam agreed. "But I know the truth. And so do you."

Garth shook his head in frustration and disbelief. "You're wrong, Sam."

"Just don't plan on seeing Callen again," Sam said baldly.

"I'll see my daughter when and where I choose."

"Not if I say no. I have some influence with my wife. She won't be working for you anymore, just so we have that straight."

Garth heaved a frustrated sigh. "I'm telling you again, I'm not responsible for what happened to E.J." He paused before adding sardonically, "And my daughter, as you will soon discover, is a woman with a mind of her own."

Sam already had some inkling of that, but he was determined to keep Callen so busy she wouldn't have time to miss her job—or see her father, even if she wanted to. "Just stay away from her," Sam repeated. "She's dead to you."

Sam whirled on his booted heel and stalked out of the café. When he reached the covered wooden porch outside the Stanton Hotel, he took a deep breath and let it out. He was not normally a vindictive man, and the outpouring of rage he had felt toward Garth Whitelaw had left him feeling drained. It was two hours before the bank opened, and he had just walked out of the best place in town for breakfast.

He thought of going home, and an image rose before him of Callen lying tangled in the sheets on his bed. Hell, he'd just go on home and get back in bed with her. There was plenty of time to come back into town later and pay the banker. He had accomplished what he'd set out to do. There was no reason why he couldn't go home and enjoy his wife...while she still was his wife.

Four

The first time Callen's mother called to invite the newlyweds to dinner, Callen accepted on the spot. She had been spending all her time fixing up the house, waiting to see if her father would relent and ask her to come back to work at Hawk's Way. So far, he hadn't budged an inch.

"Of course, we'll come, Mom," she said. "What time? We'll be there. Sam? Oh, I'm sure he'll be free. Don't worry, Mom. We're both looking forward to it." She had laughed at the cautious note in her mother's voice. Maybe her wedding hadn't been auspicious, but her marriage was everything she had dreamed it could be.

She was astonished, therefore, when Sam informed her he had made plans to take her out that evening.

"I was hoping to surprise you." He had a sort of sheepish look on his face that melted her heart.

"I wouldn't spoil your plans for the world," Callen said. After all, she didn't want to discourage any romantic notions Sam might have in the future. "I guess I'm not used to being married," she said, wrinkling her nose. "I'll have to get used to asking first before I make arrangements that include both of us."

Callen had called her mother with their regrets. The next time her mother called, about two weeks later, Callen said, "I'll have to check with Sam. Can I call you back later tonight?"

She had brought up the subject at dinner. Sam paused only hesitantly before he said, "Sunday dinner? I don't know why not. Sure, tell them we'll come."

Callen gave him a big kiss. "Thanks, Sam. It'll make my mom so happy. And I know you'll like my dad, once you get to know him."

Only, when Sunday came, Sam had an emergency he had to take care of that precluded going to Sunday dinner at Hawk's Way with Callen. Some fence was down along the south pasture, and his prize bull had wandered onto Abel Johnson's property. Abel didn't mind, but Sam hated giving away free stud service on his bull.

"I have to get him back right away," Sam said apologetically. "We'll have to have dinner with your folks another time."

Callen called and apologized to her mother. They set another tentative date for a week later. When the following Sunday came, Sam was sick with the flu. He looked awful, and Callen hadn't the heart to make him keep the dinner engagement with her parents.

When they had been married for three months, it came as a shock to Callen when she realized that she and Sam had not yet darkened the portals of Hawk's Way. In fact, she and her parents hadn't even crossed paths. It was easy to excuse the omission. She and Sam had both been incredibly busy.

Her time had been spent turning Sam's home—now her home, as well—into a charming, cheerful place by using lots of hard work and secondhand everything. She had managed to recover the couch with an Indian print in warm Western colors and was amazed at what a little polish had done to the furniture. She had bought paintings over the years, mostly by southwestern artists, which she had hung on the walls.

She discovered gallons of a pale yellow paint in the barn, which Sam confessed he had bought more than a year ago for the house. She took it to the hardware store and had it shaken up, and began painting the outside of the house. To her surprise, when Sam realized what she was doing, he stopped his repairs long enough to share the job with her. When they were done, she had stood arm-in-arm with Sam and admired the house.

"It looks so different!" she exclaimed. "It has a sort of rustic charm—"

"You mean, it doesn't look like a dump anymore," Sam interrupted sarcastically.

"You're putting words in my mouth," Callen protested. "I only meant that now I can see the care that went into building this place. Someone meant this house to survive for generations."

"It has. And it will," Sam said in a determined voice. He was silent for a moment before he said, "Thanks, Callen. I needed to see it like this. Like it can be."

He had gone back to his work mending the barbed-wire fence. She had refocused her attentions on the interior of the house. She replaced the heavy curtains in the master bedroom with vertical blinds from a discount store so she could still block out the sun during the hottest part of the day but enjoy the sunlight in the early morning and late evening. And she had pulled up the worn linoleum in the kitchen and found a beautiful hardwood floor, which she had refinished.

She spoke often to her mother on the phone, but it had become almost a reflex to refuse her invitations. There never seemed to be time. Callen wasn't sure how much of her reluctance to accept her mother's invitations lately was a result of being busy and how much was the result of her growing awareness that Sam didn't want to have dinner with her parents.

She wasn't sure exactly when she had realized there was a problem, but the signs were blatantly evident when she finally did. Sam reacted oddly to the mere mention of her father's name. Quite simply, his lips went flat and his eyes narrowed and a muscled jerked in his jaw. She could have gone alone to have dinner with her parents, but she didn't want them to think she and Sam weren't getting along. Because they were.

In fact, Callen had never been so happy. Sam was a dedicated and inventive lover, and he seemed to appreciate her efforts in the house. He was easy to talk to, and even though he seemed exhausted at the end of each day, he was never too tired to spend time with her. It was an ideal marriage. Except that Sam didn't seem to want anything to do with her family.

And there was something else. She couldn't quite put her finger on what it was, except she had noticed a certain reticence in Sam whenever she tried to make plans for the future, plans that included children. He said he had enough to worry about just solving day-to-day problems. He couldn't think about a family right now. And he was right. Still, it would have been nice to dream with him.

As much as it pained her to admit it, maybe Zach had been right about Sam lacking dreams and goals. For some reason Sam didn't want to think about the future. She didn't doubt that he loved her, even though he had never said the words. But she had become more and more certain over the past three months that he was hiding something from her. She was afraid to ask him about it, afraid to burst the bubble of happiness that surrounded her marriage.

Finally, she couldn't help herself. One night after supper, she blurted, "What's wrong, Sam? Why don't you want to have dinner with my family?"

He hesitated so long that she thought he wasn't going to answer her. When he did respond, he said merely, "You know how busy the past few months have been for both of us."

But she wasn't satisfied with that answer. "Did my father say something to you . . . I mean, before the wedding?" Callen held her breath. She couldn't believe her father would have had the nerve to approach Sam and offer him money to call off the wedding, as he had done with her two previous fiancés. But she could think of no other reason for Sam to dislike her father so vehemently. If anything, Callen would have expected Sam to despise Zach. After all, Zach was the one who had confronted Sam at their wedding. But Sam's anger didn't seem to be aimed in that direction.

The longer Sam hesitated, the more frightened she became that her father had offered him money. Suddenly she didn't want to know. "Forget I asked," she said, rising abruptly and heading for the kitchen sink with a stack of dishes.

Sam followed her and wrapped his arms around her from behind. He nuzzled her nape as he said, "What brought all this on?"

She sighed. "You keep avoiding any contact with my parents. I wondered why."

"It's very simple, Callen," he said in a quiet voice. "I want you all to myself."

She was afraid to believe him because it sounded so romantic and made her fears seem ridiculous. "That's all?" she asked. "Nothing else? What about my father? Do you—"

"Let's not talk about your father. Right now, I just want to make love to my wife."

He swept her into his arms, making her laugh at his impulsiveness. A moment later his mouth caught hers in a searing kiss, and then it was too late for thinking. She decided to let the future take care of itself. She was too busy loving Sam to worry about it.

Later, lying in bed beside his sleeping wife, Sam wondered how much longer he could manage to keep Callen separated from her father. It had been an exhausting exercise to keep an eye on Garth's movements and make sure Callen was away from the house whenever he visited. He had come twice to the Double L. Both times Sam had taken pleasure in sending him away without seeing his daughter.

"Where's Callen?" Garth had demanded the second time.

"In town shopping."

"I don't believe you."

Sam had made an open gesture with his hand, inviting Garth inside. To his surprise, the older man hadn't taken him at his word, shoved open the kitchen door and stalked inside.

"Callen? Are you here?" His call remained unanswered.

Sam could see Garth was surprised by the look of the place. Garth had visited E.J. often enough to know how they had lived. So he had to be aware of all the changes Callen had made. Even though Sam wasn't personally responsible, he felt proud of what Callen had accomplished. He had been amazed himself at the changes his wife had wrought. Quite simply, she had made his house a home.

It wasn't just the southwestern landscapes on the wall, or the lack of dust and cobwebs, or the shine on the furniture. It was the way she had rearranged the furniture so they could sit in front of the fire together. The way she made him comfortable in a chair before dropping to the floor in front of him and crossing her arms on his knees and resting her chin there while she talked animatedly about her day. The way fresh flowers found their way inside, along with sunlight and the evening zephyrs.

He wondered what Garth thought of all the changes. But he didn't ask. Instead, he said, "I told you she wasn't here."

"You can't keep her away from me indefinitely," Garth replied. "If this continues much longer, I'll just tell her what you're doing."

"Then I'd have to tell her why I don't want to see you. How you tried to bribe me out of marrying her." Sam relished the pinched look on Garth's face. He had the man where he wanted him. "Go away, old man. Your daughter is lost to you. Just like my father is lost to me. I hope you suffer, the way I've suffered."

Garth's face had whitened, the grooves around his mouth had deepened. But he hadn't argued, hadn't tried to defend himself again. He had simply left.

When Sam had found himself confronted by Callen this evening, he had considered telling her about the offer of money her father had made to him. That surely would have worked to alienate the two of them. But he had decided it wasn't necessary to hurt her that way. She would be hurt enough when she learned the real reason why he had married her.

Sam slipped an arm around Callen's waist and spooned her into his groin. He felt contented. Almost happy. Except that he knew all this was temporary. So there was a bittersweet quality to his life that made his chest ache and his throat swell. He wondered how long all the changes Callen had wrought in his life would last.

His personal life had undergone as many changes as his house over the three months of his marriage. Faced by Callen's boundless energy, Sam had found himself roused from a lethargy he hadn't realized had hold of him. At least he was sleeping at night, which made it easier to face a dawn that came too early, in his opinion. Sam hadn't even realized how lonely his life had been, until Callen filled his evenings with talk of her plans for the future.

He has no dreams, no goals.

Zach's words had come back to haunt Sam often in the first months of his marriage, and he had been forced to acknowledge the truth of them. There had been a time, long ago, when he had dreamed big dreams. He had imagined himself escaping the loneliness of his life at the Double L by playing football for a pro team, traveling and meeting fancy women and living the high life. He had been fast on his feet and determined to succeed.

But that dream had been blown away with the cartilage in his right knee. He hadn't been a good student and going to college for the sake of an education—rather than to play football—hadn't appealed to him. After high school he had returned to what he knew—ranching.

He was a good rancher; he understood his business. But with a whirlwind like Callen around, Sam realized just how slow-paced his life with E.J. had become. It wasn't a matter of being lazy, exactly. He'd simply had no reason to work harder. He and E.J. had always had enough for their needs, and their needs had been simple.

All that had suddenly changed with E.J's death. Callen was a big part of Sam's reawakening. He couldn't imagine himself lingering in bed after she was up and working. But even if he hadn't married Callen, his life had been changed forever by E.J.'s suicide. He had been jolted out of his lethargy by the knowledge of how near he had come to losing the Double L. The last-minute rescue provided by Callen's fortune had made him realize he didn't want to live so close to the edge. If that meant working harder, then he would work harder.

Sam smiled wryly. The fact of the matter was, it had been necessary to work harder simply to get back to where he and E.J. had been before E.J. lost his shirt to the various swindles he had invested in. Thanks to Garth Whitelaw. Although Sam still had possession of the Double L, it was a long way from being a successful enterprise. He had begun to think and plan what he could do to make the ranch more economically sound.

He had shared his ideas with Callen at first simply because she seemed to expect him to converse with her in the evenings when they sat in front of the fireplace. He wasn't really good at making small talk, so he had hesitantly revealed his idea to start training cutting horses. He was damn near as good with horses as Callen, and it gave the ranch another source of income besides beef cattle.

"That's a wonderful idea!" Callen had enthused. Her eyes had twinkled with mischief when she said, "I'll just recommend *you* to my friends who want their horses trained, instead of Daddy."

"I don't want—"

Callen had bounced up from the floor and settled herself in his lap with her arms around his neck. "I can help, can't I, Sam? I won the junior cutting horse championship when I was sixteen, just like my mom. And I've been helping Daddy work with cutting horses since I was knee-high to a grasshopper."

"I'd planned to do the work myself."

"Of course you did," she said in a soothing voice. "Only now that you've got me, why should you have to do it all alone?"

Her words had tumbled into the deep well of loneliness he lived with and filled it up a little. He reminded himself not to get too dependent on Callen, since there was at least a chance that when the showdown came, when he forced her to choose between her husband and her father, she would choose Garth. But it had felt good to pull her close, to feel the pillow of her breasts against his chest, to feel her fingers twine around the hair at his nape, to feel her lips nuzzle his throat. His hands had tightened reflexively around her.

His conscience often warned him that he was doing the devil's work, that he would regret his efforts to take revenge against Garth Whitelaw in the way he had chosen. He fought his scruples by visiting his father's grave almost daily. Each grim sojourn stoked his righteous anger and multiplied his enmity. Those malevolent feelings festered inside him, and he had to work hard to keep the darker side of himself hidden from his wife.

He had seen in Callen's eyes that she knew something was still bothering him, even though she had recently allowed herself to be assuaged with the excuse that he just wanted them to have some time alone. Sometimes he wondered what he would say to her if she probed the situation further. But she had seemed content to let the matter rest.

Until today.

It had been a bad day all around. Sam had discovered two of his steers dead from eating crazyweed. A flash flood had taken out a whole section of fence. The valves on his pickup had finally ground to a halt and needed to be replaced. Then, when he got home, he had found the kitchen torn apart and no supper ready because Callen was repapering the wall.

"What the hell do you think you're doing?" he demanded.

"It's only remnants I found on sale at the hardware store," she said, apparently assuming the source of his anger was concern about the cost of what she was doing. "Isn't it pretty?"

For the first time, he looked at the paper. It had small, multicolored flowers on a white background. No man would be caught dead putting something like that on his kitchen wall. For the space of a heartbeat he wondered how he would be able to bear looking at it if she left him. The thought made him angry. Why the hell should he care if she left him? He didn't love her. Had never loved her. Would never love her.

"It's fine," he said flatly. And then felt like a worm because her face fell.

"You don't like it."

"I didn't say that. Hell, Callen, it's great paper. I just had a horrible day. And I'm hungry."

"Of course you are," she said, immediately stopping what she was doing to come and give him a hug.

He couldn't help himself. He hugged her back. Well, hell! What was he supposed to do? He had to make sure the woman kept on loving him, didn't he?

"I'll cook," he offered. "You're busy."

She wrinkled her nose and laughed at him. "I've tasted your cooking. Give me a minute and I'll have something ready for us. You've got time to finish writing out those bills that need attention." She turned him toward the kitchen door and gave him a little shove toward his study.

He stomped off to his office—which now contained an antique rolltop desk—to work on his books, something he hated because he could never get the numbers to come out right. It was a job E.J. had always done. Which only reminded him of how much he missed his father. Now he was forced to confront the computer in the study and all those numbers. He hated numbers.

It wasn't long before he could smell something good cooking in the kitchen. Shortly after that, Callen called him in to supper. He gratefully turned off the computer and headed for the kitchen. When he got there, he stood in the doorway and stared at the table.

The wallpaper mess had miraculously disappeared. There were flowers on the table, and she had lit candles. He didn't know where she had found the china, and he was afraid to ask. The table had a cloth and cloth napkins. He couldn't remember the last time he and E.J. had put a cloth on the table, and they hadn't used candles except when the electricity went out in a storm. He had complained once that all that special stuff wasn't necessary, but Callen had told him it was no trouble at all.

He sat down with a grunt of expectation, his nose lifting for the scent of whatever it was she had on the stove.

"I just broiled some steak, threw a couple of sweet potatoes into the microwave and steamed a little broccoli on the stove."

He wrinkled his nose. "Sweet potatoes?"

"Don't you like them?"

"At Thanksgiving. With lots of brown sugar and marshmallows."

"Try one. If you don't like it, I won't make it again."

He realized suddenly she had taken the meat of the sweet potato out of the shell, mixed something into it and stuffed it back in again. "What's in here?" he asked warily.

"Cheese and bacon."

Sam grunted doubtfully, but he took a bite and found it delicious. He didn't tell her liked it; he simply ate it all without further complaint. He had to admit that Callen was a good cook. The steak was rare, the way he liked it, and the broccoli was crisp, but not raw.

He looked up when he had finished to find her watching him expectantly. "Good" was all he said.

From the smile on her face a person would have thought he had told her she was the greatest cook in Texas. He felt guilty for his faint praise and added, "Really good."

"Are you feeling better now that you've filled your stomach?"

He thought about it a minute and chuckled. "I guess I am."

"Remind me to keep you well fed in the future," she said with a grin.

There it was again. *The future.* His irritation rose at the reminder of what he was doing with her... to her... and the words were out before he could stop them. "I'm not a child, Callen. Don't treat me like one."

He saw from the stunned look on her face that she hadn't expected him to lash out at her. The hurt look that followed a moment later made him feel guilty, because he knew she didn't deserve his criticism.

"What's wrong, Sam?" she said in a voice that was threatening because it was so serious. "I want to know. I can't live like this, knowing that something's eating you inside. What is it? Please, tell me."

At first he was terrified that Garth might have told her the truth. That she was going to create a showdown here and now. He realized in a horrified instant that he would do anything to keep her with him.

Even forego your vengeance?

He avoided answering the question, reasoning that she couldn't know the truth. Otherwise she would have confronted him with it. He met her gaze, which was dark and somber.

"Sam, please. Tell me what's wrong."

He rose so abruptly the ladder-back chair fell with a crash. "There's nothing wrong with me. I'm just not used to having someone around all the time asking me dumb questions!"

She jerked as though he had slapped her. And he had, figuratively. But the Callen he knew was full of guts and gumption, and she didn't disappoint him. She jumped to her feet and snapped right back, "I'm not *someone*, I'm your *wife*. And I only want to help!"

"I don't need your help," Sam said in a harsh voice, admiring her even as he pushed her away. "I have to handle this by myself."

"Is it your father? Are you still grieving?"

"I don't want to talk about this!" Sam said, heading for the privacy of his office. Damn, if the woman didn't get to the kitchen door before him and bar the way!

"You're not leaving this room until you tell me what's wrong," Callen insisted.

"Get out of my way, Callen."

"No."

He stood there a minute, trying to decide what was best. The solution to his problem was simple when it finally came to him. He turned on his heel and headed for the kitchen door that led outside. He slammed it on his way out.

It occurred to him much later that he was going to have to face Callen eventually, or end up sleeping in the barn. When it came down to it, he decided sleeping in the barn wasn't such a bad idea after all. Maybe a night spent on her own would convince Callen that his business was his own.

Actually, Callen spent the night sleeping quite soundly. Because, while she hadn't gotten Sam to tell her what his problem was, she now knew it hadn't been her imagination. Something serious was bothering him, other than the situation with her father.

She was certain that Sam would have no choice except to confess. She wasn't going to give him any peace until he did.

Sam slept poorly in the barn. The hay in the loft was scratchy, and the wool blanket he had laid over it smelled of horse. It was also miserably hot. Sweat dribbled its way across his skin like many-footed worms. And he missed the feel of Callen lying next to him. In the hours he spent lying awake, listening to the rustling movements of the animals below, he thought about his confrontation with Callen.

He was going to have to tell her something. Otherwise she was going to ferret out the truth. He didn't want that to happen. He crept back into the house at dawn only to find his wife already fixing breakfast. He shifted his eyes to the wallpaper and said contritely, "I'm sorry. I guess I owe you an explanation."

The fool woman dropped the spatula in the pan and walked right into his arms. She felt good and smelled sweet and her mouth was warm and wet and made his body go hard.

"I missed you," she whispered in his ear. She rubbed her cheek against his jaw and made a kittenish sound in her throat that drew his body up tight. "You need a shave, Sam," she said with a raspy chuckle. At the same time, her hands came up to caress his cheeks, and she sought his mouth with hers.

A moment later she jerked herself free. "The bacon!"

He watched her race back to the stove where the bacon had kept right on cooking.

She turned back to him with a grin. "It's perfect. Sit down and eat. Once your stomach is full, there'll be plenty of time to talk."

He took her at her word. The eggs were perfectly done, over easy with the yolks soft. The bacon was crisp, but not burned, and the toast was lavishly buttered. The coffee was hot and strong. She was a darn good cook.

She waited for him to finish his second cup of coffee before she reminded him that he had a confession to make.

"All right, Sam. It's time to talk. I want to know what's been bothering you."

He took a deep breath and let it out. He had to make this good. "I—I can't do the bookkeeping."

"What?" There was a blank look on her face. Clearly she wasn't expecting anything that simple.

"E.J. used to do it. I can't seem to get the numbers to come out right, but I can't afford to hire someone else to do it. Things are in a mess."

Her whole face lit up. "Why didn't you just say so? I can do the bookkeeping for you." She lowered her lids so he couldn't see her eyes. "I mean, if you want me to."

He hesitated, as though reluctant to agree. He hadn't realized he was going to be killing two birds with one stone. Not only had he put her off the scent about his "problem," but he was also going to be relieved of the onerous task of keeping the Double L books.

"I suppose that would be all right," he said gruffly.

She left her chair and sat herself in his lap, draping her arms around his shoulders. She looked deep into his eyes, until he was sure she would see the truth. But all he saw reflected back to him was her concern.

"Don't feel bad about the bookkeeping," she said earnestly. "Some people are inclined that way and some aren't."

He felt himself flushing. She was obviously aware that he hadn't been a good student. She had said, in as gentle and caring a way as she could, that it was all right if he couldn't handle the difficult stuff. She would do it for him.

Sam had known from the first grade that he and numbers didn't get along. Reading hadn't been any easier. It had been a struggle to keep up with his class work all through school. He had been the butt of a lot of cruel teasing, and he had grown a thick skin to fend it off. E.J. had kept him from feeling like a total idiot by reminding him that he grasped most ideas readily. Thank goodness he had been fast on his feet. That had given him self-esteem and a value to his peers.

But here it was again, that insidious feeling of inadequacy, just because he found numbers more than a mere challenge. Because he found numbers impossible to understand.

He felt like shoving her off his lap, but she forestalled him when she leaned her head on his shoulder trustingly and relaxed in his arms. She trusted him. She loved him. She didn't care that he couldn't figure numbers.

The crisis was past. They could go on as before.

He let the hurt go and held her close.

Five

When Callen brought up Sam's figures on the computer she saw right away why he hadn't been able to make them balance. Several of the numbers were juxtaposed. Instead of $312.42 for fence posts, as was stated on the invoice, Sam had inserted $321.24 on the computer. It was a simple matter, once she realized the problem, to correct the numbers and make them balance. She then wrote out checks and signed them.

It occurred to her that Sam's problem with numbers might have a source he hadn't recognized: dyslexia. Only, she couldn't imagine how he could have a problem like that and not have had it diagnosed a long time ago. The more she thought about it, the more convinced she became that Sam's difficulties in school might have stemmed from his inability to see numbers and letters as they appeared on the page.

She confronted him the next morning at the breakfast table with her suspicions. "Sam, do you have dyslexia?"

Sam stared at her as if she had accused him of having a social disease. "What?"

"Dyslexia. You've heard of it, I'm sure. Letters get jumbled up on a page when a dyslexic tries to read them. It's more common in males than females. I just thought, since you had so much trouble in school..." Callen's voice faded as Sam's features reddened. Was he embarrassed? Did he think she thought less of him because he had difficulty reading? It wasn't his fault. People were born with the problem. "I just thought you might have been diagnosed with it sometime in the past."

"I'm not sick, Callen," Sam said in a terrible, low voice. "I'm just not as smart as other people."

"How can you say such a thing!"

"Because it's true," he said flatly. "I've accepted it. So should you." He rose abruptly from the breakfast table and stalked toward the door.

She rose and started after him. "Sam! Wait! I only thought—"

He turned on her, a storm of emotions on his face. He grabbed her by the shoulders and shook her once. "Let it be, Callen. I've lived with the way I am for thirty-six years. It's a little late to be coming up with excuses for why I can't manage simple, ordinary addition and subtraction, don't you think? Accept it. I'm not smart. I never promised I was."

He paused a moment and a muscle jerked in his jaw before he said, "Maybe you should have listened to your brother. I never got past high school, and I was lucky to make it through that. You don't have to find excuses for me, Callen." And then, bleakly, "I know what I am. And what I'm not."

A moment later he was gone, and she was standing alone in the kitchen wondering what had gone wrong. She had never seen Sam so angry. Or so frustrated. She had never realized he was so sensitive about his education or his intelligence. He was wrong, of course. There was nothing stupid about Sam Longstreet. He was sharp as a whip. After what she had seen on the computer, she was willing to bet he was merely dyslexic.

Only, if he was, why hadn't someone—one of his teachers early on, or the tutors Zach said the football team had hired to help Sam pass his academic subjects—discovered the problem? More to the point, how was she going to get Sam to agree to a test to determine whether he had a reading dysfunction or not?

The problem got pushed to the background when Sam returned home hobbling later that afternoon. His face was ashen, and his body was trembling.

"My God! What happened?" Callen exclaimed as Sam lowered himself gently to a kitchen chair.

"I got stomped by a cow. Made the mistake of getting between her and her calf while I was repairing some fence. I managed to slide to the opposite side of the barbed wire, but not before she laid into me some."

"Why didn't you go straight to the hospital!" Callen exclaimed as she dropped to one knee in front of him. She reached up to unbutton his torn and dirtied shirt and hissed in a breath of air when she saw the growing bruises on his chest. "Sam, this looks serious," she said in a wobbly voice. "Please let me take you to the hospital."

"It's too expensive," he said flatly. "Besides, I've been through this before. I've got a broken rib, maybe two. The most a doctor can do is bind me up. I can do that for myself."

Callen was terrified that Sam might have internal injuries he wasn't aware of, or that one of those broken ribs might puncture a lung. "Please," she begged.

"No, and that's final." He tried to get up, but groaned and slid back into the kitchen chair. "You're going to have to bind me up. I can't do it myself."

"I can't—"

"I've got bandages I've used in the past. They're under the sink in the bathroom. Go get them."

Callen found several rolls of Ace bandages where Sam had told her to look and brought them back to the kitchen. Sam had slid his shirt off his shoulders. The skin was scraped raw in several places, and the bruising looked terrible. She bit her lip to keep from pleading with him again. In the short time they had been married, she had learned how stubborn he could be. There was no sense wasting energy arguing. She would bind him up, put him in bed and then get a doctor to come see him, whether he liked it or not.

The color was returning to Sam's face by the time Callen finished. "Do you need help getting to bed?"

"I think I can manage."

When he tried to get to his feet, he swayed dizzily. He reached out for her, and she slid herself under his arm to support him. "Just take it easy," she coaxed.

Callen eased Sam into bed and retreated to the kitchen to phone the Whitelaw family doctor. "I know you don't usually make house calls, Dr. Stephens, but Sam refuses to go to the hospital. I'm afraid he may have some internal injuries. Thanks. I'll be expecting you then.''

Sam lay in bed staring at the ceiling, disgusted at having gotten himself into this situation. He didn't like depending on Callen for anything. He had to admit she had done a good job of binding his ribs. And he would have fallen flat on his face in the kitchen if she hadn't been there to catch him. But he already felt enough in her debt for all the work she had done around the house.

He had been a changed man since his marriage, rising earlier than he had in years and working late into the night. No matter how tired he was, he had always found time to make love to Callen. He had tried to convince himself it was all part of the plan. But he realized now he had done it because he had wanted to please and impress his wife. He had wanted to earn her respect. And now here he was stuck in bed, helpless, flat on his back.

He tried rising, but his ribs hurt him too much. He didn't have any choice but to stay where he was. He had just started wondering where Callen was keeping herself when he heard her talking to someone in the kitchen. His first panicked thought was that Garth had come to visit. He gasped at the pain when he tried to rise and fell back to the bed.

''Who's there, Callen?'' he called out to her. His answer came in the form of a strange man in the doorway. One look at the black bag he carried, and Sam swore under his breath. He turned an accusing glance on Callen, who stared defiantly back at him. "I told you I didn't need to see a doctor."

"I have no desire to bury a husband I've just married," she replied tartly. "You'll let the doctor look at you, Sam Longstreet, if you know what's good for you."

Sam had to admire her daring, even if he deplored her tactics. He couldn't very well walk out on her this time, and so long as the doctor was here, he might as well get checked over. "All right, Doc. Go ahead and look. All you're going to find is a few busted ribs."

Sam couldn't stand the anxious look on Callen's face. "You don't need to stay," he told her.

"Just try getting me out of here!" she challenged with a spark in her eyes.

Sam turned his face toward the wall. She had him over a barrel and she knew it. Hell, it wasn't so bad having a woman hovering over him all concerned like this. In fact, it felt kind of nice to know she cared. "Do what you want," he said. But there was more resignation in his voice than anger.

Sam lay as still as he could under the doctor's poking and prodding, but more than once he wished Callen weren't there so he could let out the groans he had gritted behind his teeth.

"Broken ribs, all right," Dr. Stephens confirmed. "I don't like the looks of that bruising. Could be some internal bleeding. I'd like you to come to the hospital where I can do some more thorough tests."

"No," Sam said. "No hospital. No tests."

"Sam," Callen pleaded.

"No."

The doctor frowned. "If that's the way you want it, I can't force you to go. But I want Callen to check for tenderness in your belly here and here—" he pointed out the spots to Callen with his fingertips "—every couple of hours for the next twenty-four, and get you to the hospital quick if any tenderness shows up. Also, watch to make sure that bruising doesn't spread any farther downward."

"Will he be all right?" Callen asked.

"So long as he takes it easy until those ribs heal."

"How long?" Callen asked.

"No work for ten days, at least," the doctor said. "Two weeks would be better. Otherwise you take the chance of aggravating your injury."

Sam scowled. He already had more work than he could handle. This wasn't going to help things. He would get up when he was damned good and ready, no matter what the doctor said.

In that respect, Sam had underestimated Callen. She threatened dire consequences if he left the bedroom and brought his meals on a tray. Sam had never had anyone fuss over him in his life. At first he felt uncomfortable having her wait on him. He had done nothing to deserve Callen's concern, and if she knew the truth, she would be throwing bowls of soup at him, not serving them.

But, oh, how he relished the tender care his wife gave him! Callen crooned to him as she soothed his sweating brow with a cool cloth. She made delicious meals and served them to him with the newspaper, which she read to him while he ate, saving him the effort.

"Why didn't you tell me you were helping Jimmy Lee Johnson earn the money for a car?" Callen asked him one afternoon.

Sam felt the heat in his throat rising toward his face. "How'd you find out about that?"

"He came here looking for work. I thought he'd heard about your ribs, but he told me you've hired him to work for you every Wednesday."

Sam was expecting Callen to complain about the expense. He had opened his mouth to justify himself when she leaned over and kissed him hard on the mouth. He was too stunned even to respond.

"You are about the nicest man I ever met, Sam Longstreet. Not many men would hire a teenage boy to do work he could easily do himself and pay him money that he doesn't have, all to help that teenage boy realize his dream. Oh, I'm so proud to be your wife!"

She was gone a moment later, back to chores in the house. But the good feeling she had inspired—the simple pleasure of feeling good about himself—lasted the rest of the day.

Sam had hired Jimmy Lee because he had seen a lot of himself in the boy. Long ago he had eked out enough doing odd jobs for neighboring ranchers to buy his first motorcycle. It was sitting in the barn now. He hadn't ridden it in years, not since he had hurt his knee his senior year in high school. He had been forced to give it up while his knee mended. Somehow, he seemed to have outgrown it after that. He wondered if it would still run. Maybe when he was on his feet again, he would check it out.

Meanwhile, Callen only barely managed to deter her mother from coming over to help nurse Sam. "He wouldn't be comfortable," she explained. "He feels bad even letting me wait on him, Mom." It went without saying that going to her parents' home, even to attend their annual Labor Day picnic, was out of the question until Sam recovered.

To Callen's amazement and delight, her brother, Falcon, and his wife, Mara, ignored her warnings against company. They had driven to Hawk's Way from Falcon's ranch in Dallas for the Whitelaw's annual Labor Day picnic, and refused to leave without seeing Callen and Sam. They brought along Charlie One Horse, the ancient, part-Comanche housekeeper who had helped raise two generations of Whitelaws.

"Charlie!" Callen cried as she grabbed him by his gray braids and pulled him close for a hug. "I'm so glad you came to visit!"

She brought them all into the bedroom where Sam was propped up and paging through a stock magazine.

"Sam, I don't know if you've ever met Charlie One Horse. He's taken care of me since I was in diapers."

Sam shook hands and said, "Glad to meet you."

Callen was so excited, she barely gave them time to greet each other before she introduced her brother and his wife. "You know Falcon," she said, "and this is Mara, his wife."

"We've met," Sam said with a smile.

"You have?"

"Years ago," Sam said. "It's nice to see you again, Falcon. I'm sorry I can't get up, Mara. We weren't family the last time we met, so I didn't get a chance to hug you then. And now I'm stuck here in bed."

"I can fix that," Mara said with a twinkle in her eye. She leaned over and gave Sam a quick kiss on the cheek. She laughed at the possessive-jealous-chagrined look on Callen's face when she had finished.

"We brought some food from the picnic, since you couldn't come," Charlie One Horse said. He began to arrange a huge spread of food on a tray that he set in front of Sam on the bed.

"We came to celebrate the day with you," Mara said, "since you couldn't come to us."

"Callen and I will go get the drinks," Falcon said as he dragged her toward the kitchen. Once they were there, he turned to her and said, "What the hell's going on, Callen? Mom and Dad said they haven't seen hide nor hair of you since you got married. I don't think they believe Sam's really hurt."

"As you can see," Callen replied in an icy voice, "he is."

"That doesn't explain why the two of you haven't been to Hawk's Way to visit since you got married."

"You must have heard some of the awful things Daddy and Zach had to say about Sam before the wedding."

"So?"

"So, in time, when things cool off, we'll go visit."

"Why can't you go now, by yourself?" Falcon demanded.

"Because I won't go where my husband isn't welcome! What if Mom and Daddy hadn't liked Mara? Or didn't want to be bothered with Susannah, because she was sick with leukemia? How would you have felt?"

Susannah was Falcon's stepdaughter, Mara's daughter from a previous marriage. Her leukemia had been in remission for four years now. Another year and she would be home free.

Falcon grimaced. "I see what you mean."

"Tell Mom and Daddy you saw me, and I'm fine. And tell them Sam really does have broken ribs."

Charlie One Horse, her brother, and his wife didn't stay long, but Callen was glad they had come.

After they were gone, however, a wave of homesickness washed over her. She missed her parents. This separation was ridiculous. She became more determined than ever to make peace between her husband and her family.

Sam continued to be an irascible patient, but Callen could see he enjoyed being taken care of even though he grumbled about it. She knew because of the way his eyes lingered on her face as she sat beside him brushing a stray hank of hair from his forehead, the way he laid his hand gently over hers as she set the dinner tray before him, the way he pulled her down to kiss her lips, sending her pulse soaring as he lazily helped himself to deep, probing kisses.

Callen only managed to keep Sam confined to bed for nine days, but during that time she learned a great deal about needing and wanting and expectation. Because, although there was comfort to be found sleeping close to his warmth, and joy in his tender kisses, both of them knew it couldn't go beyond that.

Callen had been surprised at the strength of her unrequited desire. She had never realized how much she counted on the pleasure of making love with her husband at night. She had refused to let Sam exert himself until Dr. Stephens's prescribed two weeks were up, but she caught herself dreaming about the day they could resume their lovemaking.

Callen had decided to celebrate the occasion of Sam's recovery with a housewarming party. She hadn't forgotten Zach's accusation: *Sam has no friends. You'll be all alone.* The truth was, in the months since she and Sam had gotten married, not a single neighbor had come to call. Partly, Callen assumed, it was because their nuptials had been private, and they had sent no announcements. People didn't intrude on their neighbors in the West without some indication that the visit was welcome. Callen was sure that if she had given even a hint of wanting company, she would have had it.

This was confirmed when Callen began issuing invitations for the housewarming party. She discovered Sam was admired and liked by his neighbors. They had simply respected his wish to be left alone. If Sam didn't have close friends, it wasn't because his neighbors weren't willing; it was because Sam himself had discouraged the contact.

Callen was hoping the party would be the first of many, and that she and Sam would meet other young couples with similar interests who would become their friends. She hadn't counted on Sam's strenuous objection to any kind of gathering whatsoever.

"You've done what?" he exploded. "Why the hell would you do such a thing without asking me first?"

"First of all, because I didn't think you'd mind. And secondly, because I need friends. It wouldn't hurt if you had a few, as well," she added bluntly.

Sam glowered. "I don't need anybody."

"Of course not," she said with a sardonic twist of her mouth. "However, I would like to point out that if you'd had any kind of relationship at all with your neighbors you could have called on them to help out when you got hurt."

"I don't want to owe anybody anything."

"That's clear enough," Callen snapped back. "The truth is, we all need other people, Sam. Even you."

"I won't be at any party you decide to give."

"Fine. The party's off."

Callen headed toward the parlor from the bedroom in a huff. She didn't want Sam to see how shocked and hurt she was by his refusal. She had known what she was getting into when she married

Sam. Her father and brother had both warned her what kind of man he was. *A loner. A man without friends.* She really hadn't considered what that might mean. She had seen in Sam only what she wanted to see. In love like she was, she truly hadn't minded the thought of just the two of them alone on the Double L.

Callen hadn't gone two steps before Sam caught her arm and swung her back around into his embrace. She immediately struggled for freedom, shoving against his shoulders and chest.

"Keep that up, and you're going to send me back to bed for another two weeks," he said with a groan of pain.

She stood frozen, her expression stricken. "What do you want from me, Sam?"

"I want you to listen while I apologize," he said in a quiet voice. He tipped her chin up with his forefinger and said, "Sometimes I can be a little unreasonable."

Callen arched a disbelieving brow. "You? Unreasonable?"

Sam chuckled as his arms tightened slightly around Callen. He hated the idea of exposing himself to all those people. He avoided crowds because he never showed well in them. But when he saw how disappointed Callen was, he conceded that enduring a housewarming party was little enough to give her in return for all she had done for him.

"We'll give the party," he said. "Invite anyone you want."

"Even my mother and father?"

Sam thought about refusing but realized there were ways to keep Garth from attending even if Callen issued an invitation. "Sure," he said. "Invite the whole family."

Callen's eyes welled. "Thank you, Sam. I will."

He fought off the stab of guilt clawing at his insides. The only way he could keep focused on his revenge was to remember how his father had looked when he had found him. Thankfully, Callen's voice jerked him from those grim thoughts back to the present.

"Maybe Falcon and Mara could drive over from Dallas again and bring Susannah and the baby."

"It would be nice to see them again," Sam said softly.

"Thank you, Sam," Callen replied with a shy smile. "I know you don't care much for company. I appreciate your willingness to give this a try."

Fortunately she chose that moment to kiss him, or Sam might have spoiled everything by admitting how little he was looking forward to the shindig his wife was planning.

Since it had been two weeks since Sam's injury, and they were in the bedroom, both Sam and Callen let themselves enjoy kissing and holding each other, knowing that their desires could finally be fulfilled.

It was amazing, Sam thought, how much he had missed those carnal sounds Callen made in her throat. He loved how she arched toward him, how she gave that little sigh as he sank himself into her to the hilt. He had forgotten the feel of her fingernails gripping his buttocks and the way her teeth nipped at his shoulder when she came.

Callen was astonished at how easily Sam could arouse her. How he knew just where and how to touch her so that she felt cherished and appreciated. She loved the way he kept his own desire leashed until she was satisfied and gloried in the unrestrained passion that caught him unawares so he cried out her name at the moment of climax. She lay beside him, her body heaving, feeling sated and happy.

Her hand drifted lightly across Sam's chest, her fingertips playing in the dark curls. "Are you all right?" she asked in a lazy voice.

"Mmm, hmm."

"I take that to mean you're fine," she said, feeling the smile grow on her face. She reached up a hand to trace Sam's lips. He was smiling, too.

"I love you, Sam."

Callen waited, but Sam didn't say the words back. She had her hands on his lips, so she felt the smile disappear, felt the lips flatten.

"Sam?"

Sam knew the smart thing to do was say the words, even if he didn't mean them. Somehow, he couldn't do it. Callen deserved better. He wasn't going to lie to her any more than he already had. She had to know he admired her, that he was grateful for everything she had done to make his house a home, that he loved making love to her. Wasn't that enough without the words?

He kissed the fingertips she held against his lips, and when she would have withdrawn, he reached out to catch her hand and hold it there. "You're a very special woman, Callen," he murmured against her fingertips. "I've never known anyone like you."

It was the truth, but so much less than he knew she wanted to hear. He knew it was enough when he felt her relax against him. He ignored the voice that told him he needed her arms around him at night. He was a man who had never needed anyone.

Callen tried to tell herself it didn't matter that in four months of marriage Sam had never said "I love you." He had shown he cared in a dozen different ways, not the least of which was making love to her every night. They had their whole lives in front of them. She knew in her heart that someday the words would come.

She moved forward with her plans for a lavish housewarming party, inviting all their neighbors and her entire family. Mara and Falcon promised to come again and bring the baby, whose name was Cody, and Susannah. Both Zach and her parents had also agreed to be there.

When Sam heard that Callen's parents had accepted their invitation, he made a point of seeking Garth out at the Stanton Hotel Café.

He walked up to the breakfast bar and said to Garth, "I want to talk to you. Privately."

Garth rose and the two men walked into one of the hotel meeting rooms that was empty.

"I got the invitation to your housewarming," Garth said when they were alone. "My wife and I are planning to attend."

Sam shook his head. "You're not welcome in my home." For the first time Sam saw pain flash across his father-in-law's features. He knew he ought to be gloating, but he found there was nothing to be proud of in what he was doing. He wasn't finding the satisfaction he had yearned for when he had set out upon this course. He forced himself to focus on the image of his father in death. That gruesome portrait produced the anger he needed to proceed with his vengeance.

"If you show up at my door," Sam threatened, "I'll make a scene the likes of which this county has never seen. I'll make damn sure everyone knows your part in E.J.'s death."

"You're bluffing," Garth said.

"Try me."

"I want to see my daughter."

"I want my father back."

The air sparked with electricity as the two men measured one another. At last Sam said in a guttural voice, "We don't always get what we want. Do we, Garth?"

Garth hadn't believed Sam could do it, that he could so effectively cut him off from contact with his daughter. But Callen had been a married woman for nearly four months, and he hadn't once seen or spoken to her. That seemed impossible to him, given the fact all he had to do was pick up the phone to talk to her or drive a few miles to be at her front door. But it was Callen herself who had asked both her parents to keep their distance. Garth had respected his daughter's wishes, never dreaming that so much time could go by without any contact between them.

He missed her. He wanted to see her, to speak to her, to reassure himself that she was as happy as Candy said she was from their conversations on the phone. "What if I come anyway?"

"If you insist on trying to get your daughter back, I'll give her back. In fact, I'll throw her out."

"You wouldn't do that."

"Wouldn't I?" Sam stared at Garth with eyes that looked totally merciless, with features that were as hard and unyielding as granite.

Garth knew from calls Callen had made to her mother that she was more in love with Sam now than she had been when they married. It would break his daughter's heart if Sam rejected her now. He couldn't do anything that might jeopardize his daughter's happiness. But he wondered how Callen could love this misguided and vengeful young man.

Much as Garth wanted to force a confrontation, he felt that waiting Sam out was a better alternative. Time was on his side. The chances of him running into his daughter in town or at church, or catching her on the phone, were very good. And after all, his ranch and Sam's bordered each other. There was always the possibility he would run into Callen on the range.

"You win," he said to Sam at last. "I'll find a reason to stay home from the party. I assume you have no objection if my wife attends?"

"None at all."

"If we're done, my coffee's getting cold." Garth left Sam standing alone in the empty room.

Sam wondered why he didn't feel more triumphant. He had won. He was keeping Callen and her father apart. If he wasn't mistaken, he had wounded his adversary. There had been suffering visible on Garth Whitelaw's face. He knew the expression because he had worn it himself. But he felt was no satisfaction in his accomplishment.

Sam knew what had marred his victory. It was the thought of the disappointment he would see on Callen's face when she realized her father wasn't coming. It was the knowledge of how unhappy he would be making his wife while he punished her father.

For a moment, a brief, flickering instant of time, he considered giving up his revenge. He considered forgiving Garth Whitelaw for his daughter's sake. He considered letting go of the past and grabbing for a future with Callen.

Then he saw his father in his mind's eye, lying in a pool of blood. And remembered the vow he had made.

"I promised you vengeance, Dad. And it's vengeance you'll have."

Six

Callen had several projects she wanted to accomplish before the housewarming party. First and foremost, she wanted to investigate further into whether Sam had dyslexia. A friend who was an elementary schoolteacher referred her to a woman who worked with dyslexic children. The specialist asked Callen to get a sample of Sam's writing for her.

Callen asked Sam to make up a list of his favorite foods. He was reluctant to write them down for her at first, but she insisted she was just too tired to write herself. She did her best to look weary when he eyed her suspiciously. He laboriously wrote a list, which she was surprised to see included a couple of dishes she had made for him since their marriage. The spelling was atrocious, and some of the words didn't make any sense at all. Callen was careful to keep her expression neutral when she took the list from him.

She met with the specialist and handed over Sam's list. "Is it dyslexia?" she asked anxiously.

The specialist, Mrs. Moran, smiled reassuringly. "It looks like a classic case. See? Some of the words are backward. For instance, *can* is *nac*. Are you sure someone hasn't told him before that he's dyslexic?"

Callen shook her head. "I guess when he couldn't read, the teachers gave up on him. And knowing Sam, he would have hidden the problem as best he could. Is there something that can be done?"

"Oh, yes. Some very bright people have been dyslexic and performed exceptionally well. Einstein, for example. Sam can be taught to recognize words for what they are, even backward. But it takes practice. Do you think he would be willing to work with me?"

Callen smiled ruefully. "The question is whether you'd be willing to work with Sam."

"I've got Monday and Wednesday evenings open. I can come to your house, or Sam can meet me at the school. Some of the local service clubs have gotten together to sponsor a fund so my services are free to whoever needs them."

Callen felt her heart racing with excitement. Her first inclination was to race home to Sam with the good news. Then she had second thoughts. What if he got angry when he found out that she had tricked him into giving her a writing sample? What if he didn't want any help dealing with his dyslexia? With the party only a day away she didn't want to start an argument with him. It would be soon enough to talk with him after the party about Mrs. Moran's conclusions and her offer of help.

"I'll be in touch with you," she told the specialist. "And thank you very much!"

The day of the party dawned bright and sunny, and Callen was nearly bouncing with excitement like a teenager on her way to the prom. Sam had never seen her so euphoric. "It's just a party, Callen," he said with a laugh after she tried putting both feet in the same leg of her jeans.

"I know. But it's the first party we've had as husband and wife. I want it to go well."

"It will," Sam reassured her as he dragged her back across him on the bed and nuzzled her neck playfully. "You've got every detail planned, right down to how we're going to get everyone out the door after it's all over so we can come in here and make love."

Callen grinned. "At least I planned the best for last."

Sam chuckled, then pressed his lips to her throat and began to suck.

"Sam Longstreet, don't you dare give me a hickey!" Callen half shouted, half laughed. She shoved at his shoulders, but he held her tight in his arms. "I bought a new dress and it'll show," she warned.

Sam stopped what he was doing, but didn't let her go. "I want every man there to know you're mine," he said. "I want to put my mark on you."

"You're the only man I want," Callen said in a husky voice. "The only man I'll ever want."

Sam felt a lump of emotion in his throat. How had she become so precious to him? How could he have gotten himself into such an impossible dilemma? He couldn't give her up; he couldn't give up his vengeance. What was he going to do?

"I…" He couldn't say "I love you." It wasn't fair. Not when he was using her the way he was.

"You what?" Callen said in a teasing voice.

"I bought some fancy new clothes to wear tonight."

Callen sat up, her legs draped across his waist. "You did? Oh, Sam, that's great!"

"I didn't want you to worry that I'd turn up looking like I did at our wedding."

"I never thought—"

He covered her mouth with his hand. "You know damn well that's exactly what you thought," he said with a grin. "I couldn't miss the shaving cream you stuck by the sink, or the boot polish that turned up on the back of the toilet seat, or the fact that you've ironed every single one of my shirts for the past week. And I adore you for it."

The words had come out before he had a chance to stop them. He didn't miss the startled look in Callen's eyes, or the way his own heart missed a beat when he said the words that were so close to what he knew she wanted to hear. He lowered his hand from her mouth, his gaze never leaving hers.

"Oh, Sam," she said. "Oh, Sam."

She was too choked up to say any more, and since his throat had closed like a vise, he used his hands and mouth to confirm what he had said. He cupped her breasts and felt the marvelous softness of them before mouthing her through the thin white T-shirt she wore. Her cry of delight made his groin tighten. Since he was naked under the sheets, it didn't take long before her jeans were off and he had her beneath him. He was lost in a world of pleasure so vast he wasn't sure he could ever get enough of it.

It wasn't until much, much later that Sam realized he hadn't used any protection. He had taken that responsibility from the first, because he knew the dire consequences that would result if he got

Callen pregnant. This time he had been caught up in the powerful emotions of the moment, wanting and needing to show Callen how much he cared, how much he valued her. Birth control had been the farthest thing from his mind.

Sam couldn't imagine any other woman than Callen having his children. Only now was not the time. The game hadn't yet been played out. He told himself the chances of her getting pregnant were slim to none. But he felt his gut wrench when he realized that the possibility existed.

He forced it from his mind as he and Callen finished the party preparations together. She hadn't decorated the house so much as filled it with candles and flowers. She had polished every surface and vacuumed every speck of dust. Even he was impressed with the results.

He was quite literally stunned when he saw Callen's dress for the party. He had never seen her wearing anything so sophisticated or elegant. It was a black dress that molded her figure, cut just low enough to reveal a hint of cleavage, but not enough to really show anything. The back, however, was cut to the waist, revealing an expanse of skin so enticing he couldn't keep himself from reaching out to touch her skin.

"You're so beautiful," he said in amazement.

Callen blushed with pleasure at the look of admiration and pride in Sam's eyes. "Thank you, Sam. May I return the compliment?"

"I'm beautiful?" he said with a wry twist of his mouth. He looked down at the starched white tuxedo shirt and bolo tie he wore with a black leather vest and black trousers. "It's the clothes," he said flatly. "I look like one of those rhinestone cowboys that sit around drinking tequila in a bar back east."

Callen laughed, a tinkling sound that skittered down his spine and right back up again to catch him in the throat.

"It's not the clothes," she said. "Although I must say you're looking very fine tonight. It's you," she said as she eyed him from head to toe. "You really are quite a handsome man, Sam. I can't believe I never saw it before."

He felt himself flush at the compliment. She was looking at him as if she would like to eat him whole. Sam felt his body respond quickly and fiercely to her invitation. He kept himself a foot away from her, knowing that if he touched her they wouldn't be dressed to greet the guests that were due any minute. But he couldn't take his eyes off her, and he knew from her face that she was feeling the same need he was to wrap himself up in her and never let go.

They both jumped when they heard a knock at the door.

"Party time," Sam said, his voice harsh with desire.

Callen cleared her throat. "Shall we greet our guests together?"

Sam slipped an arm around her waist and drew her close. "Let's go."

The rest of the party was a nightmare for Sam.

He recognized their first guests as Tom Swan, who had been the center of the high school football team, and his wife, Julie. The two had been inseparable since sixth grade. Tom shook Sam's hand and greeted him with a friendly smile that Sam made himself return.

But Sam wasn't seeing Tom's smile or hearing his greeting. He was remembering the day in high school when he had overheard Tom talking to several members of the team in the locker room, while they thought he was in the shower.

"That Sam," Tom had said. "He sure can run! It's just too damn bad he can't read!"

He heard the boys he had thought were his friends laughing with hilarity at what a dumb jock he was. Oh, he had been a riot, all right. He could still feel the awful aching pain of that betrayal.

Looking into Tom's clear blue eyes, Sam knew his former teammate's opinion of him hadn't changed. Except now he couldn't run, either.

Tom was just the first of several of his high school football cronies that Callen had dredged up. It seemed people stuck around this part of Texas when they were born here.

And there was Janice Reese. She was the girl he had fallen head over heels in love with in sixth grade. He had followed her around for several weeks before she turned and confronted him.

"Why are you following me around, Sam?"

"I was just wondering, Janice, if you'd go to the Halloween dance with me."

She had wrinkled her nose at him in a way he thought particularly endearing. "What makes you think I'd go out with a dummy like you?"

He had been so shocked at the bluntness of her statement that he hadn't been able to come up with a good reason why she should want to spend time with him. He had backed away and kept to himself after that.

He wondered if Janice remembered that fateful encounter. He had never forgotten it. He had known he had trouble with schoolwork, but had never associated that deficiency with anything lacking in himself. Until Janice had called him a dummy. It was amazing how that single sentence changed his perception of himself. He began to question himself, his intelligence.

He remembered asking E.J. if there was something wrong with him. But his father had reassured him that aside from having trouble reading and with figures, he was smart enough.

"Who was it figured out a way to get that windmill working again?" E.J. had said. "Who was it figured out the spring mechanism for the stall doors in the barn? Who was it figured out that mixing feeds would increase the yield of weight on the cattle? I could name a dozen other bright ideas you've come up with. You've got brains, boy. Never doubt it."

Only he had. It had come as a relief in seventh grade when he realized he could run like the wind. It had given him a way to excel at something. It had given him self-esteem. Until he had heard what the other boys really thought about him. It wasn't enough that he could run, when he couldn't read.

He had kept strictly to himself after that. He heard what his teammates said then. He was too stuck up to spend time with them now that all those universities had come courting, wanting Sam Longstreet to sign on the dotted line to play football. He had let them think the worst of him because there was no way he could tell them the truth.

And here they were, all of them in one place, smiling and shaking his hand and acting as if everything was perfectly normal. He felt sick to his stomach just being in the same room with them. They pretended like they didn't remember how it was. But he had never forgiven or forgotten their cruelty.

There was some respite from the horror of confronting his past. Surprisingly, it came in the form of Callen's two brothers, Zach and Falcon. Zach grudgingly shook his hand.

"I can see Callen's happy," he said.

"And that makes everything all right?" Sam asked.

"Just make sure she stays that way," Zach said.

Sam could see the respect in Zach's eyes, and the challenge. He couldn't help liking the other man.

Falcon greeted Sam with his arm around Mara, who was holding a blanketed baby. Susannah, her shiny black hair hanging to her shoulders, held trustingly to his other hand.

Sam remembered Susannah from their meeting years before. At the time, Susannah had been wearing a small red hat to conceal the fact that chemotherapy had made all her hair fall out. He could see the years had been good to her.

"You've got a good-looking family there," Sam said.

"Thanks," Falcon replied. "I don't have a free hand, or I'd shake yours."

"I can shake his hand, Daddy," Susannah said, suiting deed to word.

Sam bent down and shook the little girl's hand. "You probably don't remember me, but we met in Dallas about four years ago."

She frowned. "Yes, I do. You're the nice man with green eyes. I met you the day Daddy bought my pony."

Sam smiled. "I don't think I've ever been described so agreeably."

"You've done wonders with this place," Falcon said, looking around at the improvements, which he had missed seeing in his previous brief visit.

"All the credit goes to Callen. She's the one who worked the magic."

"Where is she?" Falcon asked. "I want to say hello."

"I think she's in the kitchen with your mother."

"Is Dad with them?"

Sam worked to keep his features even. "Your father couldn't come. Some kind of emergency at the last minute, I think."

"That's too bad. I think we'll try to find Callen, if you'll excuse us."

Sam looked around his parlor at the happy, smiling people and felt alone. He wanted to be with Callen, but he knew her family was with her now. He couldn't very well go in there and drag her away from them. He searched for someone, anyone he could comfortably converse with. His gaze stopped on Janice Reese.

As though he had summoned her, she walked toward him.

"I've been hoping I'd get a chance to talk with you this evening," Janice said.

"What have you been doing with yourself?" Sam asked. "I'm afraid I haven't kept up."

"I'm the librarian in town."

Sam smiled. It was more of a smirk. No wonder he hadn't seen her in nearly fifteen years. He wouldn't be caught dead in a library. It was full of books he couldn't read.

"I wondered where you disappeared to after high school," she said.

"Oh? Why is that?"

"I've had a crush on you for years. Ever since the sixth grade in fact."

Sam stared at her, stunned. "You called me a dummy!" he blurted. His face flamed.

She laughed sheepishly. "Isn't that awful? I can't believe I was so mean to you! I liked you a lot. I just . . . I was a stupid twelve-year-old." She smiled and said, "I'm sorry now I didn't track you down."

"Are you flirting with me, Janice?" Sam asked incredulously.

"Would it work if I did?"

"Nope. I'm happily married." What an easy lie that was to tell. He *was* happy. But for how long?

"That's what I thought. I could see the moment I caught sight of you and Callen together that you're in love with each other. I'm happy for you, Sam."

She lifted herself on tiptoes to kiss him on the cheek. To keep her from falling when she lost her balance, Sam slid an arm around her.

At that moment Zach turned around and saw him. He watched Zach's eyes narrow and knew he had misconstrued the situation. Callen's brother was at his side before he could even steady Janice on her feet.

"What the hell do you think you're doing?" he raged at Sam.

"Mind your own business, Zach. This doesn't concern you."

"When my sister's husband has her arm around another woman who's kissing him in plain sight of all their friends, I'd say that's my business," Zach retorted.

"Nothing happened here," Janice began to explain.

"Keep out of this, Janice," Sam said in a curt voice. "Leave us alone, please." He gave her a little shove toward the other side of the room. Once she was gone, he turned his attention back to Zach. He could see there were already a lot of eyes on the two of them. The thought of explaining himself to Zach irked him, but he didn't want to make a scene and spoil Callen's party, so he said, "That was completely innocent."

"I'll bet."

"Janice was giving me a friendly kiss, and she lost her balance. That's all there was to it."

"You bastard. How long have you been seeing her?"

"What?"

"Everyone knows you had a thing for Janice Reese when you were kids. You mooned over her for most of junior high school."

Sam stared at Zach. He hadn't imagined he had been that obvious. He swallowed over the bile at the back of his throat and said, "I haven't seen Janice for fifteen years until tonight. And I didn't invite her, Callen did."

"You expect me to believe that?"

"It's the truth!" Sam shot back. "But then, you Whitelaws aren't too big on honesty yourselves, so maybe you don't recognize it when you see it."

"What's that supposed to mean?"

"Ask your father," Sam snarled.

Sam had forgotten discretion in the heat of the moment. He was suddenly struck by the silence around him and turned to find everyone staring at him and Zach. What he saw in their eyes made him furious. How dare they judge him! How dare they condemn him! Then he caught sight of Callen's stricken face in the kitchen doorway.

She looked embarrassed and ashamed. Of him.

And why shouldn't she be? They all knew what he was. Dressing up and putting on airs didn't change the fact he was dumb as an ox.

He shoved a hand wearily through his hair and turned his back on all of them. "Go home," he said quietly. "The party's over."

He heard shuffling and muttering behind him, heard Callen's voice thanking them all for coming. Heard her reassure Zach and Falcon and her mother that she would be fine. That she was in no danger.

Oh, but she was! She was deeply embroiled in his plan to ruin her father. He hadn't cared whether she got destroyed in the process. And now it was too late. She was going to be hurt. And there wasn't a damn thing he could do about it.

You could give up your vengeance. You could forgive Garth Whitelaw and go on with your life.

"Sam?"

He turned around and saw Callen standing not a foot away from him, her eyes filled with concern. Everyone else had gone.

He shoved his hand through his hair again. "I'm sorry, Callen."

"What happened, Sam? I thought everything was going so well. Why did you start a fight with Zach? Why did you ask everybody to leave?"

"Zach started the fight," he retorted. "And I asked them to leave because I didn't want them here."

"Why not?" When he didn't answer, she reached out a hand and laid it on his chest. "Please tell me, Sam. I want to understand."

He brushed her hand away because he wanted so badly to hold her in his arms when he knew he didn't deserve the love she offered him.

"Don't you see?" he said in an agonized voice. "They all knew."

A frown furrowed her brow. "Knew what?"

"About me."

She shook her head. "You're going to have to be more specific than that. Knew what about you?"

"That I can't read a third-grade primer. That I could barely get through high school. That I couldn't get into college if I tried. That I'm not smart." An agitated hand went forking through his hair again. "Hell. That I'm dumb as ditch water."

"You listen to me, Sam Longstreet! You *are* dumb if you think I'm buying that hogwash for one single minute. You're plenty smart. Your problem is you're stubborn as a mule."

"Oh, Callen." He drew her into his arms, unable to keep his hands off her another second, and hugged her tight. "Saying I'm smart doesn't make it so."

She freed her hands and cupped his face, forcing him to look at her. "There's nothing wrong with you that can't be fixed, Sam. The truth is, you have a reading disability."

"Callen—"

"Shut up and listen to me!" she said. "You have dyslexia, Sam." He started to let her go, so she slipped her hands around his neck and hung on tight. "I checked with a specialist. I gave her that list you made for me. You aren't dumb, Sam, you just see numbers and letters all jumbled up on the page. Einstein had dyslexia, Sam. It has nothing to do with intelligence."

His face flushed a ruddy color. "Callen..." He was afraid to believe what she was saying. Afraid to hope.

"You're a darling idiot, but you're *not* dumb," Callen repeated, looking earnestly into Sam's green eyes. "Mrs. Moran—she's the specialist—says she can teach you how to overcome your reading problem. I told her you'd want to try. Will you, Sam?"

"Callen..." His voice was hoarse and his nose stung. He felt like crying. "It's too late—"

"It is not too late! Mrs. Moran says all it takes is time and effort."

"I don't have the time," Sam said flatly.

"Make the time."

"I'm too old—"

Callen put her hand against his lips to shut him up. "You can learn to read, Sam. You can learn to add and subtract. It isn't going to be easy. And it might even be embarrassing at your age. But if your willing to make the effort, you can resolve a problem that's obviously been bothering you for a lot of years. I'll do whatever I can to help, but really, this is something you're going to have to do yourself."

Sam could hardly force the words over the thick lump of feeling in his throat. "What if I fail?"

Callen's arms tightened around him, and her lips pressed against his in comfort, in reassurance. "You won't fail, Sam. I firmly believe you can do anything you set your heart and mind to do."

Sam had to turn his head away so she wouldn't see the tears in his eyes. His voice was gruff with feeling when he spoke. "All right, Callen. If you want me to, I will."

She began pressing light, loving kisses all over his face.

"If we're done talking, I think it's time for bed," Sam said. "We can clean up this mess in the morning." He lifted Callen in his arms and headed for the bedroom.

He made love to her almost desperately. He wasn't sure what was driving him. Fear. And elation. What if he could learn to read, after all?

He had listened to Callen's offer of help from Mrs. Moran as though it were no big deal. But deep down, in some secret hidden place where he had stuffed all the shame he had felt as a boy growing up, unable to do simple things like read or add a column of figures, a hard knot began to loosen.

Seven

————

Once Sam started working with Mrs. Moran, his progress was astonishing. Even Callen was amazed at how quickly he mastered his reading disability. Not that it was easy. And it was embarrassing at times. Callen saw his frustration on occasion, when the words on a page simply made no sense to him. But with an objective in sight, Sam devoted himself wholeheartedly to learning.

Having tackled one challenge, Sam was ready for another. His hope of making the Double L into one of the finest cutting horse ranches in Texas was about to begin.

The first cutting horses arrived two weeks after the housewarming party. Sam and Callen worked together training a sleek quarter horse mare for a rich client in El Paso who wanted to give it to his daughter as a birthday present.

When they began to work with the mare, Callen saw a facet of Sam she hadn't known existed. He had an understanding of animals, a rapport with them, that was transcendent. She had great skill maneuvering a cutting horse; Sam became one with the animal.

"Why haven't you been training cutting horses all along?" Callen demanded when Sam stepped down from the saddle after working the mare. "You're absolutely brilliant!"

One corner of Sam's mouth cocked up in a self-deprecating smile. "You think so?"

"Absolutely! I've never seen anybody ride like that, and I've seen a lot of competitions in my day."

Sam shrugged. "I've always had an affinity to horses." He paused and added, "Animals don't care whether you know how to read."

"Oh, Sam." Callen stepped into his arms and hugged him tight.

"It doesn't hurt so much anymore," Sam admitted quietly. "I mean, now that I know what was wrong. I suppose it's going to take a while getting used to the idea of picking up a newspaper just like other folks and paging through it. And I don't imagine I'll ever take up reading for pleasure." He grinned charmingly. "But I won't ever feel like I'm less smart than another man, ever again. I have you to thank for that, Callen."

"Someone else would have pointed out the problem if I hadn't come along."

"No one else ever did."

How long, Sam wondered, would he have remained blind to the truth if Callen hadn't come into his life? In a matter of months she had turned his life upside down. If he held on to his goal of revenge, he might eventually ruin hers.

"Sam, I met a young woman when I was in the hardware store having some wood cut for shelves. She seemed really nice. Her name is Natalie Folsom. Her husband, Ted, is the new agricultural extension agent. I'd like to invite them to dinner."

"Are you asking me for permission, or telling me what you've done?" Sam asked.

Callen grinned. "You know me too well. Actually, I invited them for Saturday night. I'm willing to call and cancel if you don't think it's a good idea."

Sam sighed. He would probably never be a gregarious person, but it was foolish to let his past keep him from enjoying the present or the future. And Ted and Natalie Folsom weren't from around here.

They knew nothing about him. "I think it might be fun to have dinner with another couple."

The Sam Longstreet who greeted the Folsoms at the door was the man Callen had fallen in love with. Only he was clean-shaven, had his chestnut hair trimmed above his collar, and wore polished boots and a pressed Western shirt and jeans. Callen hadn't let Sam's appearance keep her from falling in love with him, but she had to admit she felt proud of the man standing beside her.

Sam felt like a different man. It wasn't just his spiffed-up clothing and appearance. The difference came from the inside. He felt more self-confident, more sure of himself. Frankly, there wasn't anything different about him except that he knew now he was dyslexic. He had a learning disability, not an inability to learn. And he was making up fast for lost time.

Natalie Folsom was a curly haired redhead, with hazel eyes that crinkled when she smiled, and a smile that took up most of her face. She was petite and looked about seventeen, even though she admitted to twenty-four. Her husband, Ted, was only a few inches taller, but he had a muscular build. He wore glasses and had a receding hairline, but his face was open and friendly. He admitted to being a wrestler back in college ten years before, which made him a year younger than Sam.

They had nothing in common, Sam thought as the evening wore on, and yet he liked Ted. He was a good listener, and he made interesting comments when he spoke. Natalie was funny, and Sam loved seeing Callen laugh at her jokes.

Then Sam mentioned he had a motorcycle.

Ted's eyes lit up. "You have a motorcycle? What kind?"

Sam grinned. "Harley-Davidson, what else?"

"A Hog? Really? Me, too," Ted said. "Can I see it?"

"It's in the barn, covered with a tarp. I haven't even looked at it for years."

"Then don't you think it's about time you did?" Ted asked.

The four of them traipsed out to the barn, and Sam pulled a dusty canvas tarp off his Harley-Davidson touring motorcycle.

Ted whistled. "What a beauty! You've had a lot of custom work done. I'll bet all this chrome sure shines up nice."

Sam reached out and slid a hand along the leather seat. "I'd forgotten how much I liked this machine." He had spent hours working on it, tuning it, shining it. He had been lost in a world of his own.

"Sam, I didn't even know you owned a motorcycle," Callen said. "When can I get a ride?"

"You want to ride it?" Sam asked in surprise.

"I'd *love* to ride it," Callen said with a sparkle in her eyes.

"How much work would it take to get it ready?" Ted asked.

Sam shrugged. "It shouldn't take much. I put it away clean."

"Then how about if we all take a ride next Saturday, let the wind blow in our hair and the bugs catch in our teeth."

Sam grinned at the picture Ted had conjured. "Sure, why not?"

"We can take along a picnic," Natalie said.

"And I know just the spot where we can go," Callen offered. "If this very late Indian summer cooperates. Who'd have thought it would still be warm this late in November?"

That night, as they lay in bed together after making sweet, sweet love, Callen laid her head on Sam's chest and slipped an arm across his waist and snuggled close. "Did you like Natalie and Ted?"

"Yeah. They're nice." Sam was feeling good. He couldn't remember a time when he had been this contented. He wondered what it was going to be like, having a friend like Ted. It had been easy talking to the other man, easy to share stories about their Harley-Davidsons. And he owed it all to Callen. She was the one who had met Natalie and invited the other couple to supper.

"You don't mind getting together with them again?" Callen asked.

"Hell, no. I'm looking forward to it. I can't believe we're going to a picnic on motorcycles," Sam said, grinning in the dark.

"Me, neither," Callen said with a giggle. "It almost makes me feel like a kid again."

"I'll bet you were hell on wheels," Sam said.

"Wait'll you see me on Saturday," she promised.

"I can't wait," Sam said as he turned and kissed her.

He wanted her again. Incredible as it seemed, he was hard and ready. They were both already naked, so it was easy enough to lever himself over her, spread her legs with his knees and thrust into her.

"Sam." She moaned his name as she arched beneath him. "Oh, Sam."

He kissed her with joy, with thanksgiving, with the love he felt but could not speak aloud. He wasn't supposed to care. She was merely a means to his vengeful ends. But he showed her with his mouth and hands what he truly felt in his heart.

Sam spent every spare moment of the next week working on his Harley in the barn. Callen always knew where she could find him. Once they made love facing each other on the leather seat. Once, when she wore a skirt, he stripped off her underwear, then unbuckled his belt, unzipped his pants and took her standing up against the wall of the barn. Once he took her to the loft and laid her down on a blanket in the hay. They made love often, with joy in their hearts. Life seemed perfect.

Then Callen's mother called to invite them to Hawk's Way for dinner.

"Next week is the beginning of the Christmas season, and it dawned on your father and me that we haven't seen much of you lately." The truth was, Callen and her father hadn't exchanged a word in nearly six months. "We'd both love to see you. Can you come?"

"I'll have to talk it over with Sam. But I'm sure we'll be able to come," Callen said.

"That's wonderful! We'll look forward to it. Call us when you know for sure."

Callen felt her stomach do a little twist when she hung up the phone. She had been so very happy before her mother reminded her that Sam and her father didn't get along. Well, she had tackled every other problem in her marriage with determination and conquered them all. What was one more little glitch? How difficult could it be to turn her husband and her father into friends?

"No," Sam said. "I'm not going to set foot in your father's house. Not now, not ever."

"Why not?" Callen demanded, her fists perched on her hips. "This has gone on long enough. I want to know what you have against my father."

Sam's lips pressed flat. He had known this moment was coming, that it would arrive sooner or later. He just hadn't expected it so soon. He met her brown eyes evenly and said, "Your father is responsible for E.J.'s death."

She got so deathly pale he thought for a moment she was going to faint. He reached out for her, but she flinched away from him.

"That's impossible. Your father committed suicide."

"Do you know why my father took his life?"

Callen frowned. "Not exactly."

"E.J. invested his life savings and every bit of capital we had for running the ranch in several get-rich-quick schemes. They turned out to be swindles. He lost everything. We were going to lose the Double L. He couldn't live with knowing he'd lost the only thing he had to pass on to me. So he killed himself."

"I still don't see where my father fits into that picture."

"Your father advised E.J. to make those investments."

Callen shook her head no, slowly at first and then more vehemently.

"Shake your head all you like. E.J. never made a financial move in his life that didn't have Garth Whitelaw's stamp of approval."

"My father wouldn't have advised E.J. into anything that wasn't legitimate. Not on purpose."

"Oh, he did it, all right. And I even know why."

"All right. Why?"

"He wanted Double L land to replace what he gave away to Zach on his twenty-first birthday."

"That's ridiculous!"

"Is it? Think about it. How many times have you heard your father wish he had back the land he gave to Zach?"

Callen sucked in a breath. She had heard her father say exactly that over the years. He had given Zach thousands of acres of Hawk's Way land, in fact, about the same amount of acreage that comprised the Double L. And of course he missed the land, because it meant he couldn't run as many cattle, didn't have as much land to grow feed, didn't have the same lines drawn on the vast map of Hawk's Way that hung over the mantel in the parlor.

Her eyes widened in fright and horror. She didn't want to believe Sam's accusation. Refused to believe it. And was horrified to realize how much Sam must hate her father if he believed what he was saying.

"How could you marry me, thinking that about my father?" she asked in a quavery voice.

"I didn't intend to share you with him," Sam said. "I thought we'd never have to see him again."

"But he's my father!" Callen protested. "I love him. I could never stop seeing him!"

"Not even for me?"

Callen paced the room like a restless animal in a cage. "I love you, Sam. But I can't stop loving my father because I love you."

"And if you had to choose between us?"

Callen turned horrified eyes on Sam. "You wouldn't ask that of me. Surely you wouldn't!"

Here it was. The moment of truth. If he had done his work well, Callen would choose him over her father. Garth Whitelaw would realize exactly what price he had paid for coveting Double L land. He had lost his chance to have the land. Now he would lose his daughter, as well.

"I am asking, Callen. I'm asking you not to go to dinner at Hawk's Way. I'm asking you not to see your father again."

Callen stood still, but her whole body trembled. "I'm going, Sam. What you're asking of me is unreasonable. I won't be forced to choose between my husband and my father. I love you both."

"You can't have us both," Sam said flatly.

"What do you mean?" Callen asked, wide-eyed with distress.

"If you go to dinner at Hawk's Way, don't come back here. You won't be welcome."

Callen laughed, a harsh, unnatural sound. "I can't believe what I'm hearing! And it's so funny. My father threatened nearly the same thing—that I would lose my job at Hawk's Way—when I said I was going to marry you. Sam—" She reached out a hand to him, but he stepped back beyond her reach.

"I meant what I said, Callen. The choice is yours."

Callen slept on her own side of the bed that night, hugging her arms to her body, unable to believe the impossible choice she had been given. She loved Sam more now than she had ever imagined possible. But she would die a little inside if she never saw her father again. She supposed she could concede to Sam now, and hope that he would change his mind later. But what if he didn't?

The next morning Sam noticed the air was almost as frigid as Callen's behavior toward him. "Good morning," he said as he sat down in the kitchen with a cup of coffee. One sip of the stuff had him screwing up his mouth at the bitter taste.

"I suppose if it gets any colder we'll have to call off the picnic on Saturday," he said.

"I'm not in the mood for a picnic anymore." Callen slammed his breakfast down in front of him.

The yolks on the eggs were broken and cooked hard, and the bacon was burned. Sam's lip curled. The woman sure knew how to make a subtle point.

She plopped down in the chair across from him and settled her fisted hands on the table in front of her. "Sam, we have to talk about this. You've got to change your mind."

"No." The eggs stuck in his throat. He washed them down with a sip of bitter coffee.

"Have you talked to my father? Did he give you any explanation of what might have happened?"

"I don't need to talk to your father. I know what I know."

"You're a damn fool, Sam," Callen accused, rising to her feet, "if you assume facts without knowing them."

Sam flushed. "I know my father, Callen. He wouldn't have done anything so foolhardy as investing on his own. He knew his limitations."

"So my father's to blame? Have you ever considered that your father may have made those decisions all by himself? That my father may be entirely innocent?"

Sam had refused to consider that possibility for several reasons. First, he knew how much his father had always relied on Garth Whitelaw to advise him on his investments. Second, if his father had made those decisions on his own, then it meant he was entirely responsible for losing his fortune, and that he had taken the coward's way out by committing suicide and leaving Sam to face the consequences alone.

Sam didn't want to believe that about his father. He needed to believe E.J.'s misfortune could be laid at Garth's door, along with the responsibility for E.J.'s untimely death.

"Do you want me to call Ted and cancel the picnic?" Sam asked.

Callen thought about it a moment. She had made up her mind to attend the dinner with her parents at Hawk's Way. If Sam held to his threats, she wouldn't be seeing him again after that. The picnic with Ted and Natalie might be the last one they ever had together. She wanted that memory to take with her.

"Tell them to dress warm," she said.

Sam couldn't believe that Callen was sticking to her guns. The dinner with her parents was the following Sunday. If he couldn't convince her to stay, he was going to have to let her go.

He was terrified of losing her.

He visited E.J.'s grave three times in the next week. He sat there with his back resting against the headstone and spoke aloud to his father, venting his frustration and asking for advice. He picked one of the fall flowers Callen had planted there and twirled it in his fingers. Then he began plucking the petals.

"She loves me . . . she loves me not . . . she loves me . . . she loves me not . . . she loves me. I really think she does, E.J. And I love her. I'm not exactly sure how it happened, but I think I've loved her for a long time. I don't know how I'll live without her. It's killing me to do this. But I don't know any other way to pay Garth back for what he did to you. And I promised you I'd give you that satisfaction, at least. It'll hurt him for sure if he knows Callen is suffering because of him. And I think she will, if I force her to stay away from the Double L.

"But, oh, God, Dad. I don't want to do it! It's tearing me apart inside. Tell me what to do! Tell me how to make everything come out right!"

There were no answers from the grave.

The day of the picnic dawned sunny and brisk. Sam produced a black leather jacket for himself and one for Callen. On the back in red lettering were the words Born To Be Wild.

"Where did you get this?"

He held it for her while she slipped into it. "I bought it for you. I thought we might start riding together."

She kept her chin down and her lashes lowered so he couldn't see her face as she zipped it up. Sam had bought this jacket when he thought they had a future together. If he didn't change his mind, this might be the only time she ever wore it.

Callen had ridden horseback all her life, so she knew the thrill of having a lot of horsepower between her legs. But when Sam revved up the Harley and she sat down behind him with her arms circling his waist, she knew what it was like to fly without ever leaving the ground. She felt the wind in her hair and smiled, knowing the chance she was taking that she would end up with bugs in her teeth. It was glorious.

It took a lot of trust to sit behind Sam and let him direct their course. She felt the power of the machine and the man who controlled it. She would have followed Sam anywhere, she realized. She knew he wasn't perfect. Far from it. But then, who was? Where it counted, when it counted, she knew Sam would always be there for her, loving her.

"Having fun?" Sam shouted over his shoulder. The wind caught the sound and sent it in all directions.

With a helmet on, Callen heard nothing. "What?"

"Having fun?" he repeated.

"Yes. I don't ever want to stop," she hollered back.

"What?" he shouted.

"Never mind," she said in a normal voice. "I know the trip is almost over. I just want to enjoy what there is left of it."

They ended up at the entrance to a deep canyon where there must once have been water since several cypress and cottonwoods had grown there. The weather was brisk, but there was no wind, and the bright sun made it seem warmer than it was.

Callen spread a blanket and the two women put out a picnic fit for kings. "Come on, fellows," Callen called. "Time to eat."

Callen and Sam never referred to his ultimatum once all day. They chatted with their new friends and discovered that all of them like to do the Texas two-step. They made a promise to go dancing together as soon as they could find a time when they were all free.

Sam and Ted talked about the weather and the price of cattle and whether interest rates were going to stay down or go back up again. Callen and Natalie talked about the weather and the price of food and whether health care reform would ever become a reality.

After lunch, when the sun was at its warmest, Ted and Natalie decided to take a walk down into the canyon.

"I'd rather rest, I think," Callen said.

Sam looked sharply at her. His Callen *resting?* It was unheard of. "Are you all right?"

She smiled lazily. "I'm just fine. A little tired. I didn't get much sleep last night."

Sam knew at least one worry that might have kept her awake. "You two go on," he said to the other couple. "We'll wait for you here."

Sam set himself down on the blanket with his back against a cottonwood and patted his thigh. "You can use me for a pillow."

Callen scooted over so she could rest her head in Sam's lap. "Thanks, Sam."

They didn't talk. Both of them knew it would have meant arguing. By tacit consent, they were determined to enjoy these last moments together before all hell broke loose.

To Sam's surprise, Callen fell asleep only minutes later. He brushed her bangs away from her face, then smoothed his thumb across her cheek for the sheer pleasure of touching her skin. He wanted to hold her close and never let her go. He wanted to treasure her. He wanted to get his children on her. He knew he had created the tense situation between them, and that he had the power to end it.

Sam leaned his head back against the tree and stared up through the branches into the cloudless blue sky. How important was vengeance, anyway? An eye for an eye, a tooth for a tooth, the Bible said.

He needed to see Garth pay for E.J.'s death. Needed to know his father's death had been avenged, so he could finally lay E.J. to rest. So he could go on with his life.

But what kind of life did he have to look forward to if he lost Callen in the pursuit of his almighty vengeance?

He convinced himself, sitting there under a leafless cottonwood, that in the end she would choose him over her father. After all, she loved him. And she wouldn't want to hear her father say "I told you so." She wouldn't leave him. She couldn't.

Sam hadn't realized he had fallen asleep until he heard the quiet murmur of voices. Maybe he hadn't slept so well himself last night. He slowly opened his eyes.

Callen was sitting nearby talking to Natalie. Ted was over by the cycles, polishing chrome. He realized Callen was talking about him, about their marriage. He quickly closed his eyes, curious as to what she would say.

"I can't believe you actually went through with the wedding," Natalie exclaimed. "If Ted had shown up looking like that, I'd have bolted for sure."

"Sam isn't the sort of man you should judge by appearances," Callen replied. "It's what's on the inside that really matters. He's kind. And hard-working. He makes me feel special. And he's so very smart."

Sam struggled not to wince at that. It was taking time for him to accept himself the way Callen insisted upon perceiving him. He remembered a boy struggling to make sense of confusion on a page. She saw a man with dyslexia who had accepted the challenge to read.

"And I know Sam will make a good father," Callen said.

"Are you by any chance expecting?" Natalie asked.

Callen didn't answer, and Sam held his breath. She must have gestured one way or the other with her head, but by the time he opened his eyes a slit, she had resumed speaking.

"There's only one problem with Sam," she said.

"What's that?" Natalie asked.

Sam clenched his teeth. Well, this was it. She was going to tell Natalie about their argument, about his ultimatum.

"He drives way too fast on that motorcycle!"

Sam exploded with laughter.

"Sam! How long have you been awake?" Callen demanded.

"Long enough," he said with a grin. He rose to his feet. "Come on. I think it's time we headed back.

I'm going to need lots of time to get home before dark, if I don't want to drive too fast.''

He held out a hand and Callen took it. He dragged her to her feet and into his arms and gave her a lusty kiss.

Callen struggled only a moment before she kissed him back. When they finally separated, she scolded him. ''What will Ted and Natalie think?''

''That I like kissing you. And you like kissing me back.''

Callen's cheeks were tinged with rose by the time Sam finished kissing her a second time. ''It's getting dark, Sam. We'd better be heading back.''

Sam saw the sun was on its way down. This idyll, indeed, the halcyon days of their marriage, were nearly over. Whether Callen left him, or whether she stayed, things would never be quite the same between them again.

Callen spent the entire week leading up to the first Sunday in Advent arguing with Sam, trying to convince him that he was being unreasonable. But he was adamant. On the Saturday before she was to have dinner with her parents, she brought out the big guns. She let the tears drip in cascades from her eyes, even though she knew she never looked her best when she was crying. Desperate situations required desperate measures.

The tears almost did him in. Sam was torn in two at the sight of Callen's tear-streaked face. He wanted to say the hell with it and let her go. Only he turned at that instant and spied a small stain on the hardwood floor where E.J.'s blood had soaked into the aged wood. He had covered the spot with a rug, but the rug had slid away to reveal the dark secret beneath it. His heart hardened. He had sworn vengeance against Garth Whitelaw. By God, he would have it!

At last the fateful day arrived. In the stark morning light, from the rumpled sheets he had shared with his wife the night before, Sam watched Callen dressing for dinner with her parents at Hawk's Way. "So you're going, after all."

"Yes."

She looked awful, Sam thought. Her eyes were red-rimmed from all the crying she had done, and there were shadows under her eyes that told him she hadn't slept. Hell, neither had he. He wasn't about to miss a moment of what might very well have been the last night his wife spent in his bed.

"I don't want you to go, Callen."

"Don't you see I have to, Sam? They're my parents. If E.J. were still alive, would you avoid him simply because I didn't like him?"

Put that way, his request did seem unreasonable. But the whole crux of the problem was that her father was the reason his father was dead. And if he wasn't able to keep Callen away from Garth, then he would have to put the other part of his plan into effect. He would have to do his best to make Callen miserable, and force Garth to live with the knowledge that he was the source of his daughter's unhappiness. He had to cut Callen out of his life. He had to divorce her.

Sam could see she was ready to go. "If you leave this house, don't come back," he said in a voice that sounded like a rusty gate.

"You don't mean that," Callen replied in a calm voice.

Her eyes were full of love for him. He felt like a band was tightening around his chest, cutting off his air. He stopped breathing entirely when he heard what she had to say next.

"Because if I go out that door, never to return, so does your son or daughter." Callen closed the bedroom door with a quiet click behind her.

The silence was deafening.

An instant later Sam was out of bed and had his jeans on. He zipped them halfway up and skipped the snap. They barely clung to his hips as he headed after her. "What did you say?"

Sam caught Callen in the kitchen and dragged her back around to face him. There were tears in her eyes again. He hauled her into his arms and held her there. She was going to leave him. He could feel it from the way she remained stiff in his arms, unyielding.

He hadn't figured on a child. He had used protection every time. Except that once. Just once. And there had been dire consequences for his lapse.

Sam had a decision to make. Which was more important? Vengeance? Or a lifetime with Callen and the child she carried inside her?

It was far easier to put the burden on her. He let her go and stepped back. "Don't go, Callen. Please, don't go."

"I have to, Sam." The words were wrenched from her as she turned and ran.

Sam let her go.

Eight

Garth and Candy welcomed their daughter with open arms. They exchanged a look of concern over her head as they led her into the parlor to have a glass of wine before dinner.

"None for me," Callen said. "Water will be fine."

Candy poured a glass of sparkling water and added ice before she handed it to her daughter. "Sam isn't coming?"

Callen shook her head. She turned to look out the window and blinked back a tear before it could spill.

"I can't believe so much time has passed since you got married," Candy said. "We kept expecting to see the two of you here at Hawk's Way any day. Now it's nearly Christmas."

"Yes," Callen said in a voice that was commendably calm. She had already bought one of Sam's Christmas presents. She had signed him up for an audio book club, so he could listen on tape to all the books he had never read. "There was a lot to do on the Double L. Sam and I have been very busy."

Callen was a married woman and soon to be a mother herself. If she had learned anything in the months she had been married to Sam, it was that there was no obstacle too great to be overcome. Look at everything Sam had survived. Surely there was some way to resolve this dilemma so they could all have Christmas together.

"Is Sam treating you well, Callen?" her mother probed.

"Obviously her husband isn't treating her right," her father muttered. "Otherwise she wouldn't look like death warmed over."

"I'll thank you not to say anything disrespectful about my husband," Callen said. "What goes on between Sam and me is our business."

"I'm sorry he wasn't able to come," Callen's mother said.

"I'm just as glad he didn't," her father countered.

Callen rose and confronted her father. "I mean it, Daddy. If you make one more remark like that about Sam, I'll leave."

"Please, Garth," Candy said. "Let's just have some dinner and let Callen tell us what she's been doing since she and Sam got married."

Callen saw the warning look her mother shot at her father and was grateful for the help in steering her father away from the subject of Sam Longstreet. But it was too much to hope it wouldn't be raised again at the dinner table.

"So what have you and Sam been doing that's kept you so busy you can't—"

"Garth."

Her mother's warning cut her father off and gave Callen an opening to answer his question. She told them everything. How Sam had needed her fortune to save the Double L from foreclosure. How she had remodeled the house as best she could using items she had scrounged, or bought at a discount, or repaired with a little elbow grease and the sweat of her brow. How proud she was of the result. How she and Sam had painted the house together and how good it looked when they were done. How Sam had come up with the idea of training cutting horses and how successful they had been with a mare intended for a girl in El Paso. How she had discovered Sam was dyslexic, and how he was finally, at long last, learning to read.

Of the revelation about Sam, her mother said, "That's unbelievable. I wonder why no one ever figured it out before."

Because no one cared enough to find out the truth. Because Sam never let anyone get close enough to see how he was suffering because of it. Callen couldn't say that to her parents. They wouldn't understand. And really, it didn't matter now. She was there to love Sam, to care whether he was happy. That is, if he let her come home to him after she had finished this dinner with her parents.

She didn't tell them about the baby. She didn't want it to be used as a pawn in the battle she could see was coming. Nor did she ask her father about whether he was the one who had advised E. J. Longstreet into so many bad investments. She knew her father well enough to believe he hadn't done anything dishonest. If he had suggested some investments that turned out to be swindles, he had not done it knowingly. Besides, there was no way to change the past. What was done was done. It was Sam who had to forgive and forget.

Callen sought for a safe subject of conversation and found it. "What have you two been doing with yourselves at Hawk's Way, now that all three of your young ones have finally flown the nest?"

Her parents exchanged a tender look. Her mother flushed. Her father grinned.

"To be honest," her mother admitted, "we've had a sort of second honeymoon."

"That doesn't mean we don't want to see our children as often as they can come visit," her father said.

"I'm glad for both of you." Callen ate the last bit of apple pie that Charlie One Horse had made because he knew it was her favorite dessert and shoved her plate away. "I'm afraid I've got to go now."

"Can't you stay and visit longer?" her father said.

"I need to get home. There are lots of chores to be done. And I want to be sure I have time to cook supper for Sam."

Her parents walked her to the door, clearly reluctant to let her go.

"When will we see you again?" her mother asked.

"Soon."

"Don't make it so long next time," her father said gruffly as he pulled her into his arms at the door and gave her a hug. "I love you, Callen," he whispered in her ear.

Callen bit her lip to keep from bursting into tears. She couldn't remember the last time her father had told her he loved her. Callen hugged him hard. She peered up at him when he let her go. The skin was stretched taut over his cheekbones. He was getting older. There was more gray in his hair, and the creases beside his mouth were deeper. She glanced at her mother and saw there were lines around her eyes that she had never noticed before. Where had the time gone?

They were already grandparents to Falcon's step-daughter and newborn son. Now they were going to have another grandchild. And she was going to have to find a way to convince Sam that their child needed its grandparents.

"Goodbye, Daddy. Goodbye, Mom," she said, giving them each another quick hug and a kiss. "Don't worry about me, please. I love Sam. And I'll find a way to make everything all right."

She was gone before they could ask her what she meant.

Callen drove back to the Double L as fast as her car could get her there. She parked in back and headed for the kitchen door. She turned the knob and shoved, but the door didn't budge.

It was locked.

She banged on the door. "Sam! The door's locked. Come on, let me in."

There was no answer. She couldn't imagine why the door was locked in the first place. They never locked the doors. It wasn't necessary. She raced around the house to the front door, thinking it might be open. It was locked, as well.

She pounded on it and shouted, "Sam! I know you're in there! This is ridiculous! Let me in!"

A quick check revealed his motorcycle was gone. So, he wasn't inside listening to her pound on the door, after all.

There was a key under the mat in front, and Callen stooped to see if it was there. It was. She picked it up and stood in the fading light of dusk and stared at it. All she had to do was put the key in the lock and open the door.

Why had Sam locked the doors, but left the key, she wondered, unless he intended for her to let herself in? But if he wanted her inside, why hadn't he simply left the doors open? Why had he made sure to be gone when she got home?

Callen felt a rising fury. If Sam was backing off from his ultimatum, if this was his idea of an apology, it fell far short of what was necessary. And if he was testing to see whether she dared to come inside after he had made it clear she wasn't welcome, he was going to be sorely disappointed. If Sam wanted to play games, she would show him how it was done. He would soon discover that a Whitelaw learned in diapers how to win.

Callen's lips twisted in chagrin. Of course, there was the small matter of where she was going to stay until Sam came after her with an apology on his lips. Returning to Hawk's Way was out of the question.

She got into her car and headed down the drive away from the Double L without any clear destination in mind. Not that she could see anything anyway, for the tears blurring her vision.

When she realized several minutes later that she was on the road to Hawk's Way she pulled over to the side of the road and stopped. She refused to go home to her father. She didn't belong there anymore. She turned the car around and headed in the other direction.

She had only been to Zach's ranch a few times, but nothing had ever looked as sweet to her as his white-washed Spanish-style adobe house. She parked the car in back and headed for the kitchen. She opened the unlocked door without knocking and stepped inside. Zach was sitting at the island bar in the center of the kitchen, finishing up a supper that looked like it had gone from the freezer to the microwave. He looked up when she appeared in the doorway, startled. He rose and took a step toward her.

Callen collapsed, weeping, into her brother's comforting arms.

He didn't ask her any questions. He didn't say "I told you so." He merely put her into bed in his guest room, drew the drapes to make it dark, closed the door and left her alone.

* * *

Sam sat with his back against E.J.'s headstone. Tears had dried on his cheeks. It was nearly full dark. He knew Callen must have come home by now and found the doors locked. He wondered whether she had bothered to look for the key and whether she had used it. He was afraid to go home and find out.

He had argued with himself for hours about whether he ought to simply go back to the house and unlock the doors and welcome home the best thing that had ever happened to him. In spite of all his threats, he knew he would welcome her with open arms if she came back to him. She had to know how he felt. But he had never told her that he loved her. He had never told her how precious she was to him.

Sam tried to remember what his life had been like before Callen came into it nearly nine months ago. Bleak. Lonely.

Lately it had been filled with laughter. Soon there would be a baby crying, bringing new life to the Double L. Unless Callen saw those locked doors and left. What if she didn't remember about the key under the front door mat? What if she didn't think to look for it?

He didn't know how he would live without her.

Sam jumped up and ran for his motorcycle. He lay low along the tank as the wind whistled around his ears. He felt the fear rise as he approached the house and saw it was still dark. He raced for the back door, yanked on it and realized it was locked. He pounded on it twice in frustration before he sprinted around to the front.

He saw the shine of the key in the last rays of daylight. It was sitting on top of the mat in plain sight. She had found it. But she hadn't used it.

Sam grabbed the key and jammed it into the lock. He turned the key and forced the door open, shouting as he hurried through the dark house.

"Callen? Where are you? Callen? Are you here? Callen?"

He turned on lights as he went until he had illuminated every square foot of the house. She wasn't there.

He walked back into the parlor and sat in the chair she had scrounged for him and put his feet up on the comfortable ottoman. There was no warm fire to greet him. There was no warm woman to hold in his arms. He leaned back wearily in the chair. He had never been so tired.

Where could she have gone?

To Hawk's Way, you fool. And you have no one to blame but yourself. You had a chance. You could have made a choice.

I did make a choice.

You made the wrong one.

I owed E.J.—

Do you think E.J. would have wanted to see this happen? Do you think E.J. would want his grandchild to grow up without its father?

She'll come back.

Better if you go after her.

She'll come back.

You're a fool, Sam Longstreet.

Sam tried to find some satisfaction in what he had done. His revenge was complete. But as he looked around his empty house, bereft of love and laughter, and thought of sleeping in his bed, empty and cold, and imagined a future spent alone...vengeance suddenly didn't seem so important anymore.

It seemed a betrayal of the feelings he had for his father to choose Callen over vengeance. But vengeance was a bitter bedfellow.

Sam was torn in two. He couldn't think right now. He closed his eyes and let blessed sleep claim him.

Callen pounded on the door. "Sam! Let me in! Sam!"

The front door opened abruptly and Callen nearly fell inside. Sam caught her firmly by the shoulders and kept her at arm's length. "You left this house, Callen. You're not welcome here anymore."

She laughed shakily. "Sam, this is my home, too. You're my husband. I want to come in."

"No, Callen."

Callen was stunned. He had meant what he had said. He didn't want her anymore. And all because she refused to love one man more than another. Callen had too much pride to beg. "All right, Sam. Have it your way."

She turned and walked toward her car. She got in and gunned the engine, spitting rocks and dust as she headed down the drive.

Only she had no place to go.

"Callen! Callen!"

It was Sam. He was calling her back. He wanted her—

Callen bolted upright when she felt a hand on her shoulder. Where was she?

"You were having a bad dream," Zach said.

Oh, my God, it had all been a dream! Callen bit back a sob. The nightmare had seemed so real!

She looked around her, trying to orient herself. This wasn't her bed. There was no comforting warmth lying beside her. It all came back to her again with her eyes wide open. The awful confrontation with Sam. His ultimatum. Returning home to find herself locked out. Leaving the key where Sam was sure to find it and know she had chosen to leave him. Coming to Zach's house and collapsing in his arms.

"Oh, God."

"Are you all right, Callen? You cried out in your sleep."

It was still dark. She couldn't see Zach, but she could feel his arms close around her shoulders. She leaned her head against his chest and sighed. "I've made a mess of everything, Zach."

"You had some help."

"Yes. Sam isn't without blame. What am I going to do now?"

"Get a good night's sleep and go home tomorrow."

"It isn't that simple. Sam threw me out."

"He what?"

"He's got this crazy idea that Daddy is responsible for E.J.'s death."

"That's hogwash."

"He says Daddy pointed E.J. toward those investments on purpose, because he wanted him to lose the Double L."

"Why?"

"So Daddy could buy the Double L when it went into foreclosure and replace the land he gave to you."

Zach remained silent, and Callen's heart fell.

"I knew he wanted to buy some more land," Zach mused quietly. "But I thought he had Abel Johnson convinced to sell."

"You're not suggesting Daddy might have done what Sam's accused him of, are you?"

"No. Dad and E.J. were too close for that. I think if Dad had wanted E.J. to sell to him he would have come right out and asked."

"What if E.J. said no?"

"Then I think Dad would have looked elsewhere."

Callen sighed. "I thought the same thing. But Sam refuses to believe me. And he refuses to listen to anything Daddy has to say."

"Then I guess we'll just have to catch him and hog-tie him and make him listen."

Callen laughed at the image Zach had conjured. "Oh, I'd like to see you try."

"You think I couldn't do it?"

"I think you'd have your hands full trying."

"Seriously, Callen, what are you going to do now?"

"Can I stay here?"

"You're welcome for as long as you want to stay."

"I'll have to find a place of my own soon," she said.

"You'll be no bother here."

"Yes, but I have a feeling you may draw the line at hosting a squalling infant."

She heard Zach take in a breath.

"You're pregnant?"

"Nearly three months."

"Sam Longstreet is a fool."

"Right now, I'd have to agree with you." Callen felt like crying.

Zach must have sensed it somehow because his arms tightened around her and he ruffled her hair. "Don't worry, Callen. Everything will turn out fine. You'll see. First off, I'm going to see Dad and explain the situation. I may not be able to make Sam listen, but surely Dad can find a way to make him hear the truth."

"Oh, Zach, I hope you're right."

"You'd go back to him if he asked?"

"In a heartbeat. I love him, Zach. More than my own life. More than anything."

"Then why aren't you at the Double L right now?"

"Because Sam has to realize he loves me the same way. Until he does, until he realizes that nothing is more important than our love for each other, it's better that I stay away."

Zach eased her back down. "Get some sleep, Callen. We have a long day ahead of us tomorrow."

Zach didn't go back to his own bed. He dressed and left the house, arriving at the imposing front door of Hawk's Way a half hour later. He let himself in and made his way upstairs to his parents' bedroom. The door was closed and he knocked.

He heard the rustling of bedcovers inside and then his father's voice. "Who's there?"

"Zach."

His father and mother both appeared at the door a moment later. "What's wrong?" they said together.

"It's Callen."

"Is she all right? Has something happened to her?" his mother asked.

"She's fine, Mom. She's at my place, sound asleep in the guest room."

"If that bastard has done anything—"

"Hold on, Dad," Zach said. "You'd better be sure Callen doesn't hear you bad-mouthing Sam like that. She's likely to scratch your eyes out."

"What the hell is going on, Zach?" Garth demanded.

Zach turned to his mother. "I need to talk to Dad. Could you leave us alone for a little while?"

"There's nothing you have to say to me that your mother can't hear," Garth said.

"All right. I'll wait for you both downstairs."

It didn't take long for Zach to relate everything Callen had told him. Except the fact that she was pregnant. He figured she would rather tell them that herself. "So you see, Dad, you're going to have to make Sam listen to the truth."

"You don't think Sam's version of what happened is the truth?" Garth questioned.

"No, Dad. And neither does Callen. But I'm curious. Just what did happen?"

Garth sighed. "I believe I'll save that explanation for Sam. But I don't think he's going to want to hear it."

"When are you going to see Sam?" Candy asked.

"Is tomorrow morning soon enough?"

"I guess it'll have to be," Zach said. He rose with a stretch, and yawned. "I guess I'd better get back home and get what sleep I can. I'd advise you to do the same."

Once Zach was gone, Garth and Candy walked arm-in-arm back up the spiral staircase. They went through the motions of removing robes and returning to bed. Garth turned out the bedside lamp and pulled his wife into his arms.

But sleep wouldn't come.

"It wasn't your fault, Garth," Candy whispered in the dark. "There was nothing you could have done."

"I'm not so sure," Garth said. "He was my friend. I should have been able to prevent what happened. I should have done more. I should have done *something.*"

"You did what you could. You did more than most. Don't blame yourself."

"Sam blames me."

"Sam needs someone to blame."

"What if he won't listen?"

"He'll listen. And he'll recognize the truth when he hears it."

"I hope you're right."

"Try to sleep, Garth. You'll need your strength tomorrow." Candy pressed her cheek against Garth's chest and let her hand twine in the hair at his nape. "You're a good husband, Garth, and a good father and a good friend. Don't ever doubt it."

"Thanks, Candy. I needed to hear that." Garth pulled his wife close. She was the treasure of his life. The light that burned bright in his soul. He hoped his children found the same wonder in their spouses that he had found in his.

Garth lay for a long time staring into the dark. He felt Candy's breathing deepen and steady into the rhythm of sleep. At long last, he closed his eyes and drifted into sleep.

Nine

No doubt about it, Sam Longstreet was a changed man. And it was all the result of his marriage to Callen Whitelaw. Sam stood on his front porch, which no longer sagged, and looked around him. Not only had the rotting boards been replaced on the barn, but it had been painted a rust red. There were six sleek quarter horses in the corral, waiting to be worked. Two of those cutting horses belonged to the Double L. The rest were being trained for clients he had advertised for in quarter-horse journals. He had written the ads himself and read them when they appeared in the magazine.

He brushed a hand across his clean-shaven jaw and wiped the polished toes of his boots against the back of his jeans. There wasn't a piece of clothing in his drawers with a rip or tear, not a button missing on one of his shirts. He owed that to Callen, too.

In the distance he saw a windmill twirling like mad, but no screech of unoiled metal carried to him on the wind. He could see his cattle near the stock tank, munching contentedly on hay he had planted and reaped himself. He would be taking them to market soon, and because he was a lucky man, the price of beef was up.

The Double L had never been so profitable as it was now. He had made his mortgage payments the past few months with money earned by the sweat of his brow—and Callen's. He mustn't forget his wife when he was counting his blessings. Because she was the greatest one of all.

Sam knew what his wife had given to him. His ranch. His self-respect. Her love.

What had he offered her in return? Dishonesty. Duplicity. Deception.

He had never once told her his true feelings. Although, perhaps that wasn't surprising, since he had lied to himself almost from the first. He must have loved her even then. He couldn't remember a time when he hadn't. Only he had never told her. He had never said the words aloud. Not when she married him. Not when she made love to him. Not when she gave him back his ranch or offered him a chance to read and write when he thought such feats impossible. Not even when she made him believe there was nothing he couldn't do if he set his mind to it.

Had he made her happy, as he had promised he would on the day he proposed to her? He thought perhaps she was. Or had been, before he insisted on having his revenge against her father. If he had it all to do over again, he would do things differently. Oh, yes, he would. He would recognize the prize he had found in his wife and cherish her and protect her from anything that threatened her happiness.

He couldn't live the past again. But there was the always the future. Sam headed back inside the house for breakfast. There were no days off on a ranch. Despite everything, he had work that had to be done.

He wasn't hungry enough to cook himself a breakfast, settling for two cups of coffee while he stared out the curtained window in front of the sink. It was almost painful to be in this room without her. He wanted her here. Needed her here. Wished she were here.

Callen had lavished her attention on everything from the shiny hardwood floor to the new coat of paint on the cabinets to the flowery wallpaper. She had made the room hers, made it light and lovely. It wasn't a bachelor kitchen anymore.

Sam remembered a story Callen had told him about what it was like to grow up with two older brothers. They had gotten into so much mischief the neighbors had dubbed them the Three Whitelaw Brats. She was always tagging along behind them.

"But they didn't want me there," she said wistfully. "I was in their way. They had to be more careful when I was around—although I got hurt often enough even as it was.

"I grew up thinking I could do anything they could do. Mostly, I could. It wasn't until much later that I realized I didn't want to do all the things they were doing, that there were other things that interested me more. Only, if I did those things, I wouldn't have my brothers' company. I would have to do them alone.

"It's hard to believe that with everything I had at Hawk's Way, I could have been lonely. But I was. I was too much of a tomboy to get along with the other girls when I was younger, and by the time I realized I wanted to be just like them, it was too late. I couldn't seem to go along with the crowd. I was too much my own person.

"I spent a lot of time alone. That was what drew me to you at first, you know. I saw that same look of loneliness in your eyes. And I knew we could be friends."

"Why did you marry me, Callen?" he had asked.

"I wanted someone to love. I wanted to be loved by someone. And I wanted a home and a family of my own."

She had expected so little from their marriage. And so very, very much.

Sam's neckhairs stiffened when he heard a knock at the front door. That alone announced it wasn't a friendly visit. He made his way through the house to the front door. When he opened it, he found Garth Whitelaw standing there.

"I want to talk," Garth said. "And I won't take no for an answer."

Sam hesitated before stepping back. "Come on in and say your piece."

Garth took a quick look around and saw that more improvements had been made since the last time he had been inside. The house had a warmth and coziness that proclaimed it a home. Unfortunately, his daughter was no longer living here. It was a situation he hoped to remedy.

Garth turned to Sam and found the other man's face unreadable. Which meant he didn't detect the loathing that had been there the last time the two of them had conversed. But there was no liking evident, either.

"I knew about those investments E.J. made," he began.

Sam's hands balled into fists, which he pounded against his thighs. "Damnation! I knew it! I knew you were to blame!"

"I didn't say I was to blame," Garth corrected in a terse voice. "I said I knew E.J. invested in those deals. He came to me and asked me what I thought. I advised him against it."

"The hell you did! If you'd told him not to invest, E.J. wouldn't have invested."

Garth shook his head. "That's where you're wrong. E.J. was sick, Sam. He had prostate cancer. He knew he was dying, and he wanted to leave you more than what he had. He was hoping to make a killing, since all those deals offered a substantial return. Only E.J. got burned. I think he was afraid to face you and tell you the truth." A muscle in his cheek jerked. "Just like I was."

Sam's face had bleached white. "You're lying." E.J. sick? E.J. dying of cancer? It was all so improbable. So unbelievable. Only, Garth's words had the ring of truth.

"I wouldn't have cared if he lost everything," Sam said in a hoarse voice. "I wouldn't have blamed him. He didn't have to kill himself!"

"He was afraid of the cancer, Sam. I think that was as much the cause of what he did as losing his fortune." Garth sighed deeply. "I know it wasn't my fault, and yet I still felt responsible when I heard E.J.

had killed himself. I felt I deserved whatever scorn you heaped on my shoulders. I should have interfered. I should have argued more against those investments E.J. made. I should have made him tell you about the cancer. Maybe then..."

Sam put out a hand to stop Garth's speech. "You knew E.J. as well or better than anyone. Do you really think you could have stopped him once he got an idea fixed in his head?"

"No. You're right. He was one stubborn cuss." Garth paused and added, "And you take after him. I came here today to tell you the truth. And to tell you you're a fool if you let Callen slip through your fingers. I haven't figured out why, but my daughter loves you enough to take your side against her own father. She threatened to leave my house if I said a word against you."

"She did?" That was news to Sam.

"I suggest you get yourself on over to Zach's place and get your wife and bring her home."

"I already have."

"What?"

At that moment a sleepy-eyed, tousle-headed woman came walking into the room. She walked right into Sam's open arms.

"Hi, Daddy."

"What are you doing here, Callen? Zach came over in the middle of the night to tell us you'd left Sam and were sound asleep in his guest bedroom."

"I had. I was." She shoved her bangs out of her eyes and yawned.

"Then, what the hell are you doing here?"

"Oh. Sam came and got me." She smiled a Cheshire grin and looked lovingly up at Sam. "He near pounded the door down. I guess that must have been when Zach was gone to Hawk's Way, because when I answered the door, Sam threw me over his shoulder and carried me away. It was very romantic."

Garth gawked. He couldn't help it. "You two are crazy."

"Crazy in love," Callen said as she stared into the warm welcome in Sam's green eyes. "It seems Sam can't live without me. And of course he wanted to be around while our child was growing up." She laid a hand on her belly, and Sam put his hand over hers.

Garth grinned as understanding dawned. "I'm going be a grandfather again? That's wonderful news, Callen." He leaned over quickly and kissed her cheek. He held out his hand to Sam. "Congratulations, Sam."

Sam took Garth's hand. "I'll take good care of her, sir. You don't have to worry about that. And about the other..."

"I should have explained everything sooner."

"I should have been more willing to listen."

It was as much of an apology or explanation as either man would ever offer. They shook hands once more before Garth stepped back.

"I guess I'll be going now. Does your mother know about the baby?"

Callen shook her head.

Garth's grin broadened. "I can't wait to tell her. You can expect her to call, I'm sure."

"Tell her to make it later," Sam said as his arms closed once more around his wife.

"I'll do that."

A moment later Garth was gone.

Sam scooped his wife into his arms and headed back toward the bedroom.

"Sam!" Callen exclaimed. "What are you doing?"

"I'm taking you back to bed, where I can make love to you to my heart's content."

"That sounds like a lovely idea."

Sam knew he had made the right choice, the only choice in retrieving his wife from her brother's house. He had sought vengeance against Garth Whitelaw to salve his own hurt. It wasn't what E.J. would have wanted. When it came down to a choice between having his wife and hurting her father, Sam had known what he had to do.

Callen had made her capture and capitulation seem romantic when she related it to her father. But it had been far more difficult to convince her to come home than Sam liked to remember. In fact, he felt lucky to have convinced her at all.

"Why do you want me back, Sam?" she had demanded.

"Because I need you."

"That isn't enough. I won't be used as a pawn to hurt my father."

He had swallowed hard and said, "I love you, Callen."

"Oh, Sam." She let one sob escape before she put a fist to her mouth to hold back the rest. "If you only knew how long I've waited to hear you say those words. But it'll tear me apart to love you, if it means letting you destroy my father."

"I don't want to destroy your father. Not anymore."

He had seen the hope in her eyes. "Really, Sam? Have you forgiven him?"

"I believe he's responsible for what happened to my father," he countered. "But I'm willing to forego my vengeance for your sake."

"That's not enough, Sam."

"What do you want from me?" he had asked bleakly. "I've chosen you instead of revenge. I've chosen love instead of hate. What more can I do?"

"Stop punishing yourself for what wasn't your fault. Forgive yourself for not knowing how upset and depressed E.J. was. Stop blaming yourself for your father's death."

"It wasn't my fault!"

"I know that," Callen had soothed. "And deep down, so do you. E.J. chose to die. He was the one who was responsible. Not my father. And not you."

"Callen...I..." She had been sitting in a chair in the kitchen. He had fallen on his knees in front of her as she opened her arms to him. He had clutched her tightly and felt her arms fold around him.

He had grieved then, the bitter tears cleansing away his anger and his guilt and, along with them, the need for revenge. He was whole once more.

He had picked Callen up in his arms, and she had clung to him, sitting close to him all the way home in his pickup. They hadn't made love last night, but had fallen asleep in each other's arms.

Then Garth had come this morning and explained about E.J.'s cancer. Sam would always regret the way his father had died. But he would be able to look back now without the terrible hate and anger that had colored the past months.

As he laid Callen on the bed and slipped in beside her, he pulled her close. "I love you, Callen. More than my life. More than anything."

"And I love you, Sam. I was just thinking..."

"What?" Sam asked as he nuzzled his wife's throat.

"I know you and Daddy would really like each other if you spent some more time together. So why don't we—"

Sam shut his wife up in the time-honored way, by covering his mouth with hers. He had the feeling he was going to spend the next few years going toe-to-toe with his bride. Which wasn't such a bad fate, when he thought about it.

"Sam—"

He kissed her again.

"Sam..."

And again.

"Oh, Sam."

"I love you, Callen."

Sam grinned as he kissed his wife. At least he had gotten in the last word this time.

Epilogue

"**S**am, come quick!"

As a new father, Sam jumped two feet whenever he heard Callen call these days. Her frantic cry from the kitchen had him sprinting there to join her. "What's wrong? Are Karen and Kayla all right?"

His question was answered before he finished voicing it. His twin one-year-old daughters were sitting happily in their high chairs with cereal dribbled across their mouths, the trays of their high chairs and the floor.

"Come here and read this, Sam," Callen said, thrusting the local newspaper across the kitchen table toward him.

Sam took the paper without experiencing the knot that would once upon a time have formed in his stomach at the mere thought of confronting the written word.

"Look at that," Callen said, her finger thumping against the paper. "I can't believe any brother of mine could do anything so incredibly foolish."

Sam read the item Callen had pointed out to him.

Wife Wanted

Texas rancher seeks honest, responsible, compliant woman for wife. Must be capable of bearing children. Contact Zachary Whitelaw, Hawk's Pride, or phone 555-6748.

"Well, I'll be damned," Sam said with a chortle of glee. "That's one way to find a wife I'd never have considered."

"Do you see what that ad says?" Callen ranted. *"Compliant!* He might as well have said he wants a wife who'll kowtow to everything he says. The nerve!"

"Settle down, sweetheart. Your brother's a big boy. He knows what he's doing."

Callen snorted. "That'll be the day. The only comfort I have is that the whole idea is so ridiculous, so preposterous, that no sane woman will respond."

Sam threw the paper on the table. "I guess we'll just have to wait and see. Right now, I have more important things to think about." He drew his wife up into his arms. "You two close your eyes," he said to the little girls.

Sam lowered his mouth and gave his wife a lingering kiss, doing his best to ignore the giggles from the high-chair peanut gallery.

*   *   *   *   *

Watch for The Disobedient Bride
A Man of the Month in April 1995.

*Rebecca Littlewolf is anything but the
compliant wife Zach Whitelaw is seeking, and
wills clash when Zach finds himself married
to a spitting wildcat instead of a
tame kitten!*

Another wonderful year of romance concludes with

Christmas Memories

Share in the magic and memories of romance during the holiday season with this collection of two full-length contemporary Christmas stories, by two bestselling authors

Diana Palmer
Marilyn Pappano

Available in December at your favorite retail outlet.

Only from **Silhouette®**

where passion lives.

XMMEM

MONTANA™
Mavericks

Stories that capture living and loving beneath the Big Sky, where legends live on...and mystery lingers.

This December, explore more MONTANA MAVERICKS with

THE RANCHER TAKES A WIFE
by Jackie Merritt

He'd made up his mind. He'd loved her almost a lifetime and now he was going to have her, come hell or high water.

And don't miss a minute of the loving as the passion continues with:

OUTLAW LOVERS
by Pat Warren (January)

WAY OF THE WOLF
by Rebecca Daniels (February)

THE LAW IS NO LADY
by Helen R. Myers (March)
and many more!

Only from ❦ *Silhouette*® where passion lives.

THE BRANIGANS ARE BACK!

You fell in love with the rugged Branigan brood
before—now those brothers have returned...
sexier than ever!

Coming in January from

SILHOUETTE® Desire®

BRANIGAN'S BREAK by Leslie Davis Guccione

Irresistible Sean Branigan didn't need help raising his
two teenagers—especially from beautiful Julia Hollins!
She was driving him crazy with all her advice...*and*
with her sinfully sexy ways!

Don't miss BRANIGAN'S BREAK (#902) by
Leslie Davis Guccione—only from Silhouette Desire.

HOMETOWN WEDDING
by Pamela Macaluso

Don't miss JUST MARRIED!, a fun-filled new series by
Pamela Macaluso about three men with wealth, power and
looks to die for. These bad boys had everything—except the
love of a good woman.

Bad boy Rorke O'Neil has all the local women's hearts
racing. Yet Callie Harrison had learned the hard way
just what a wild, worldly hellion Rorke really is...but
how can she forget how wonderful it felt to be in his big,
strong arms?

Find out in *Hometown Wedding,* coming to you in
December...only from

SILHOUETTE... **Where Passion Lives**

Don't miss these Silhouette favorites by some of our most
distinguished authors! And now you can receive a discount by
ordering two or more titles!

SD#05786	QUICKSAND by Jennifer Greene	$2.89	☐
SD#05795	DEREK by Leslie Guccione	$2.99	☐
SD#05818	NOT JUST ANOTHER PERFECT WIFE		
	by Robin Elliott	$2.99	☐
IM#07505	HELL ON WHEELS by Naomi Horton	$3.50	☐
IM#07514	FIRE ON THE MOUNTAIN		
	by Marion Smith Collins	$3.50	☐
IM#07559	KEEPER by Patricia Gardner Evans	$3.50	☐
SSE#09879	LOVING AND GIVING by Gina Ferris	$3.50	☐
SSE#09892	BABY IN THE MIDDLE	$3.50 U.S.	☐
	by Marie Ferrarella	$3.99 CAN.	☐
SSE#09902	SEDUCED BY INNOCENCE	$3.50 U.S.	☐
	by Lucy Gordon	$3.99 CAN.	☐
SR#08952	INSTANT FATHER by Lucy Gordon	$2.75	☐
SR#08984	AUNT CONNIE'S WEDDING		
	by Marie Ferrarella	$2.75	☐
SR#08990	JILTED by Joleen Daniels	$2.75	☐

(limited quantities available on certain titles)

AMOUNT	$_____
DEDUCT: **10% DISCOUNT FOR 2+ BOOKS**	$_____
POSTAGE & HANDLING	$_____
($1.00 for one book, 50¢ for each additional)	
APPLICABLE TAXES*	$_____
TOTAL PAYABLE	$_____
(check or money order—please do not send cash)	

To order, complete this form and send it, along with a check or money order
for the total above, payable to Silhouette Books, to: **In the U.S.:** 3010 Walden
Avenue, P.O. Box 9077, Buffalo, NY 14269-9077; **In Canada:** P.O. Box 636,
Fort Erie, Ontario, L2A 5X3.

Name:_____

Address:_____ City:_____

State/Prov.:_____ Zip/Postal Code:_____

*New York residents remit applicable sales taxes.
 Canadian residents remit applicable GST and provincial taxes.   SBACK-DF

Silhouette®
™